SEDUCING HIS ENEMY'S DAUGHTER

SEDUCING HIS ENEMY'S DAUGHTER

BY

ANNIE WEST

First published in Great Britain 2015
By Mills & Boon, an imprint of HarperCollins*Publishers*
1 London Bridge Street, London, SE1 9GF

Large Print edition 2016

ISBN: 978-0-263-26154-7

Our policy is to use papers that are natural, renewable and recyclable products and made from wood grown in sustainable forests. The logging and manufacturing processes conform to the legal environmental regulations of the country of origin.

Printed and bound in Great Britain
by CPI Antony Rowe, Chippenham, Wiltshire

This is my 25th Harlequin Mills & Boon®
novel, and the thrill of creating these stories
hasn't diminished. It has actually increased,
because now I hear from readers
from all around the world who enjoy them.

So this one is for you—all the readers who've
taken time to pick up an Annie West story.
And especially for those who have enjoyed
them and taken the time to share that.

Thanks, too, to my lovely editor, Carly,
my wonderfully supportive family,
my dear writing friends—
you know who you are, so take a bow—
and to Ale Snape Li
for helping with the Spanish!

CHAPTER ONE

'OF COURSE YOU'LL do it. You know you will.' Reg Sanderson paused in the act of pouring a double whisky to fix his gimlet stare on his daughter. As if he could bend her to his will, like he had years ago.

Ella shook her head, wondering how any man got to be so caught up in his own importance that he didn't notice the world had altered. *She'd* changed in the years since she'd walked out. Even Fuzz and Rob had changed lately, but their father hadn't realised.

He was too focused on his business machinations. Except they were no longer just business. His latest scheme was an outrageous mix of commercial and personal.

No wonder Fuzz had run. Felicity Sanderson might be flighty and spoiled, as only the favourite child of a very rich man could be, but she was no fool.

'Don't be absurd.' Ella stared her father down,

ignoring his razor-sharp glare. It had taken years of practice to stand tall against his brutal behaviour but it came naturally now. 'This is nothing to do with me. You'll have to sort it out yourself.'

Who'd have thought Reg Sanderson would come cap in hand to his forgotten middle child, the one he'd ignored for so long?

Except there'd been nothing cap in hand about his bellowing phone call, demanding she come to his harbourside home instantly because her sister Felicity was about to destroy her life.

'Of course you're involved,' he roared, then caught himself, pausing to swallow a slug of alcohol. 'You're my only hope, Ella.' This time his tone was conciliatory, almost conspiratorial.

Ella's hackles rose, tension clamping her belly. Her father shouted whenever he didn't instantly get his way. But it was when he pretended to be on your side that you really needed to beware.

'I'm sorry.' She bit her lip, reminding herself there was no need for her to apologise. Yet ancient habits died hard. She lifted her chin. 'It's a crazy idea and even if it weren't I couldn't fill in for Felicity. I'm not—'

'Pah! Of course you can't hold a candle to your

sister. But with a makeover and some coaching you'll do.'

Ella stood tall. Once upon a time his constant references to the many ways she didn't measure up to her older sister—in looks, grace, vivacity, charm, the ability to throw on anything and look like a million dollars—had been the bane of her life. Now she knew life held more important things than trying, fruitlessly, to live up to his expectations.

'I was going to say I'm not interested in getting to know any of your business cronies, much less *marrying* one.'

Ella shuddered. She'd escaped her awful father in her teens and never looked back. This man her father so wanted to do business with would be in the same mould: grasping, selfish, dishonest. She'd met his associates before.

'I'm sure if you explain the situation he'll understand.' She got up from the white leather lounge, retrieved her shoulder bag and turned towards the door.

'Understand?' Her father's voice cracked on the word, transfixing Ella. Despite his volatile temperament, she'd swear it was the closest he'd come to real emotion in years. Even when her mother died he'd shed only crocodile tears.

'Donato Salazar isn't the sort to *understand.* You don't realise how badly I need him. I suggested marriage to cement our business ties and he agreed to consider it.' Her father's tone made it clear what an honour that was. This from a man who viewed himself as the acme of Sydney business and society.

'I need Salazar's money. Without it I'll go under and soon. Even with his money…' He looked every bit his age despite the work he'd had to keep the lines and sags of good living at bay. 'I need a *personal* tie to keep me safe. A family tie.' His tone was grim, his expression ugly, a familiar scheming look in his eye.

The idea of her father's massive wealth at risk should have shocked her. But somehow it didn't. He was an inveterate risk-taker.

'You don't trust him.' Ella stared in revulsion. 'Yet you want your daughter to marry him.'

'Oh, don't be such a prude. You remind me of your mother.' His lip curled. 'Salazar can give a woman everything money can buy. You'll be set for life.'

Ella said nothing. *She* knew her mother's worth,

and that money couldn't buy the important things in life. But the discussion was academic. Fuzz had run rather than meet this Salazar person and Ella had no intention of sacrificing herself to her father's schemes. Besides, this paragon of corporate success wouldn't be interested in having Reg Sanderson's *other* daughter foisted on him. The dull, uninteresting one who actually worked for a living.

She was ordinary, a nurse who spent her days home-visiting the sick. She had nothing in common with a corporate high-flyer. Ella turned towards the door again.

'Without Salazar's money I lose everything. The business, this house. Everything. And if I go belly up, what do you think happens to your siblings?' He paused long enough for foreboding to trickle down Ella's spine.

'What about the money for your brother's new venture?' No mistaking the venom in his tone. 'The one Rob's so wrapped up in now he's left the family business. The one supporting your sister, Felicity, and her *boyfriend*.' He all but spat the word.

Ella swung around, her pulse fluttering in her throat.

'*Rob's* money, not yours.'

He shrugged, his gaze sliding sideways. 'I…accessed some of it to tide me over.' He must have sensed her outrage, cutting her off before she could speak. 'If I go down, so do they. How do you think they'll cope when the cash to finish refurbishing their fine resort disappears?' Triumph lit her father's pale eyes.

Impotent fury blindsided her. He'd *stolen* from Rob but still expected her to help him!

Trust him to realise her feelings for her siblings was a weakness he could exploit.

She'd felt profound relief that Fuzz and Rob had finally broken from their father's slimy influence. He'd poisoned their lives too long. If they lost this chance to build something for themselves… Ella shrank inside. Rob *might* be okay; he'd shown unexpected steel in walking away from all their father offered. But Fuzz had done so little for herself. Despite her sister's air of casual unconcern Ella knew she had deep-seated self-doubts. A setback like this—

Ella stiffened her shoulders like a prisoner facing a firing squad even as everything inside screamed in protest.

'All right,' she bit out. 'I'll meet him.'

But only to explain that her sister, Felicity, was no longer part of the business deal.

It would be straightforward. What sane man expected marriage to cement a business deal?

'Here she is at last.' Her father's voice vibrated with bonhomie. 'I'd like you to meet my daughter Ella.'

For a moment longer she stood, watching the dying sun turn Sydney Harbour to a mirror of peach and copper. Then with a swift, sustaining breath she made herself turn.

'Ella, my dear.' Her father's greeting made her blink. It was the first endearment he'd ever given her. She stared blankly. Once she'd have given anything to hear him address her with approval and pleasure.

The realisation made something long-forgotten crumple inside.

He spoke again. Ella heard the name Donato Salazar and pasted on a smile. She turned to the man beside him, looking up, then up again.

Something jabbed hard at her insides, a blow that all but rocked Ella back on her feet after the shock of her father's words.

The man before her didn't belong at one of her father's parties. That was her first thought.

These events teetered on the borderline between trendy and louche. This man was too…*definite* to be either. *Elemental* was the word hovering in her head. He was like a force of nature, a leader, not one of the led.

Beautiful was her second thought.

Even the thin scar running up one cheek emphasised rather than detracted from the powerful beauty of that face.

It was beautiful in the way a remote mountain crag was, its icy peak compelling to climbers yet treacherous. In the way a storm at sea was beautiful in its lethal magnificence.

Which led to her third thought: *dangerous.*

It wasn't just his utter stillness, his total focus as he scrutinised her like an amoeba under a microscope. Or that his spare, gorgeous face was hewn of slashing strokes and planes, not a curve to be seen. Except for that thin, perfectly defined mouth that drew her gaze.

In her profession she'd seen lips curved in smiles of joy or relief, drawn tight or stretched in pain or grief. She'd never seen one like this, hinting at both sensuality and cruelty, the grooves around it all about control.

Danger. It was in the air around him, the way it thickened, alive with his presence, enveloping her, drawing her.

That beautiful hard mouth moved, articulating words Ella couldn't catch as her brain blurred. Then it curved in a smile and everything sped up, her pulse, her thoughts, her breathing.

'I'm sorry, I missed that.'

'I said it's a pleasure to meet you, Ms Sanderson.' Once more those lips curved up, but Ella knew with absolute certainty it wasn't pleasure Donato Salazar felt.

That was confirmed when she met his eyes, dark denim-blue beneath sleek black eyebrows that winged upwards. His look was assessing and… annoyed?

'It's good to meet you too, Mr Salazar.'

'Mister, Ms, there's no need to be so formal.' Her father spoke and Ella had never been so grateful for his presence. He seemed almost benign by comparison with the man beside him. 'Call her Ella, Donato. We don't stand on ceremony here.'

The tall man nodded and she told herself the perfect fall of his smooth, dark hair did *not* shine with the blue-black gloss of a raven's wing. Just as that wasn't the hint of a cleft in his chin. Or a flare of understanding in those deep-set, remarkable eyes holding hers.

The idea of being read and understood by one of her father's associates was too extraordinary to consider. She'd never fitted into Reg Sanderson's world. She'd been the cuckoo in the nest, unfathomable and uninteresting.

'Ella.' Donato Salazar's voice was deep, with a resonance that trawled through her insides, leaving her strangely empty. 'And you must call me Donato.'

Perhaps it was the gleam in his eyes, the satisfied twitch of those lips, or the fact she'd finally got over his shocking first impact on her, but suddenly Ella was herself again.

'That's kind of you… Donato.' Something in his eyes flickered and Ella felt a throb of satisfaction. He was human after all. For one stunned moment he'd seemed larger than life.

'I understand you're from Melbourne. Are you staying in Sydney long?'

'That depends—' a look flashed between him and her father '—on a number of things. For the moment I have no definite plans to return.'

Ella nodded easily, as if those plans didn't include marriage to Reg Sanderson's daughter.

That was *not* going to happen.

'Let's hope the weather stays fine for your visit. Sydney is a city to be enjoyed in the sunshine.' As if she spent her days lolling on her father's motor cruiser, quaffing champagne or indulging in long lunches.

Ella pressed a hand to her empty stomach. Fuzz had left mere hours before this party to honour the man their father wanted her to marry and Reg had summoned Ella straight from work. Typically, while there was plenty of alcohol flowing, food had yet to make an appearance.

'Ah, the weather.' Donato's tone was unreadable, his eyes serious, yet she detected a flicker of superior amusement at one corner of his mouth. 'A polite and predictable conversation starter. Will you tell me how much better it is here than in wet, windy Melbourne?'

'It hadn't occurred to me.' Ella feigned surprise to hide her annoyance. She'd had her fill of being a source of amusement for her father's sophisticated friends. Years as the ugly duckling made her prickly when patronised. 'Are Melbournians really so touchy about their weather? I thought they were more robust.' She ignored her father's glowering frown. 'But do, please, feel free to choose another conversation starter, polite for preference.'

Something glinted in Donato's appraising eyes and Ella drew herself up.

'Really, Ella—' her father began.

'No, no. The weather it is, Ella.' Donato said her name slowly as if tasting it. Absurdly, since his accent was as Australian as her own, she caught a hint of exotic foreignness, an unexpected sliver of something unfamiliar and alluring in her simple little name.

The hairs at her nape and along her arms stood to attention.

She firmed her lips at such a flight of fancy. If hearing him say her name with that appealing lilt made her giddy, how would she cope when she finally saved enough for her long-awaited holiday to South America?

'Tell me—' he leaned in and Ella caught an enticing hint of coffee and warm male skin '—since you're interested in the weather. Do you think we can expect a summer storm later? Lightning and thunder, perhaps?'

Ella looked from her father, his expression icy with warning, to the clear sky, then back to Donato Salazar with his glinting, unreadable eyes. He knew how her father was sweating on this meeting and he didn't give a damn. Ella was torn between admiration and anger.

'Anything is possible, given the right atmospheric conditions.'

He nodded. 'I find the prospect surprisingly… invigorating.' He didn't move but suddenly he seemed to loom closer, towering over her despite her borrowed heels. The air around her seemed to snap and tighten. Or was that her nerves?

Ella told herself that squiggle of response deep inside was because, at five feet ten, she wasn't used to men dwarfing her. It had nothing to do with the idea of this dark, challenging, vibrant man being *invigorated*.

The image that word conjured made her catch her breath. Since when had her imagination been so flagrantly erotic?

She had an awful suspicion he read her thoughts. Heat seeped under her skin, spread across her chest and up her throat.

Maybe she'd been working with elderly patients too long. How long since she'd been close to a virile man in his prime? One whose gaze challenged her not to react to him, even as she felt that telltale melting at her core.

'Tell me more,' he murmured, his voice like dark, rich syrup. 'What atmospheric conditions would lead to electricity in the air?'

He was toying with her.

He'd sensed her instantaneous, deeply feminine response to him—that tremor in her belly, that lush softening, and it amused him. His face was as close to bland as such a strong, remarkable face could be. Yet she *knew*. Something she couldn't name connected them.

'I have no idea,' she snapped. 'I'm no meteorologist.'

'You disappoint me.' His words were silky, his gaze fixed unwaveringly on her as if she were some curious specimen. 'Most people I meet like to talk about things they know well.'

'To show off their knowledge, you mean?'

He shrugged. The implication was clear. People tried to attract his attention. Her father was about to do it, clearing his throat ready to interrupt this conversation that wasn't going as he'd planned.

'You think I should try to impress you?' Stupid question. This man could make or break her father and, by association, her siblings. She might not need to impress him but common sense dictated she shouldn't antagonise him either.

Yet it was antagonism she felt, swirling in her blood. That and attraction. And something like fear. It was a dangerous combination.

'I can tell you—' she spoke as her father opened his mouth '—that our weather often comes from the south.'

'From the direction of Melbourne, you mean?' Donato's eyes narrowed.

'Precisely.' She angled her chin higher, refusing to look away from that intent stare. 'So if there's an abrupt change in the atmosphere from the south, a big blustery wind, for instance. Or a sudden influx of hot air…' She shrugged. 'Who knows what bad weather might result?'

'Ella—' Her father's voice promised retribution but was drowned by a sharp crack of laughter.

It reverberated around her, deep and appealing. Ella's skin prickled and shivered as if in response to the elemental rumble of thunder.

Donato Salazar had a surprisingly attractive laugh for a man who looked like he could play the Prince of Darkness with no effort at all. The trouble was laughter, the humour in his eyes and that unlooked-for smile turned him into someone far more approachable.

Her fingers tingled. She wanted—so badly she wanted—to cup his face and discover how that sharply defined jaw, that rich olive skin felt beneath her hand.

Ella swung her hands behind her back, clasping them tight together like a schoolgirl.

She shivered. Her response to this man was anything but childish. Her heart pounded against her ribs, her mouth sagging till she realised and snapped it shut. And that melting sensation had spread. Between her legs felt soft like warm butter.

Horror filled her and she stumbled back, only stopping when his laughter cut off and his gaze meshed with hers.

There it was again. That certainty he *knew* what she felt. The realisation should have mortified her. Instead it felt almost…liberating.

Ella blinked. Her imagination was working overtime. Lack of food had made her woolly-headed.

She did *not* turn into a puddle of pure lust after five minutes' acquaintance with any man.

She did *not* have some psychic connection with this stranger.

'I apologise for my daughter.' Her father skewered her with a glacial look. 'She—'

'There is no need to apologise.' Still Donato didn't shift his gaze from her. That steady look was unnerving. 'Your daughter is charming.'

'Charming?' Reg spluttered before quickly gathering himself. 'Of course, yes. She's certainly *unusual.*'

Ella might have felt grim amusement at her father's description of his cuckoo-in-the-nest daughter if she weren't so flabbergasted.

Charming?

Never in her life had she been described that way. But never had she set out to be deliberately rude either.

It was a night of firsts. Her father needing her. Her visceral response to this tall, dark, enigmatic stranger.

If there were going to be many more surprises maybe she should grab a drink to steady her nerves.

'You must be proud of such an intelligent, forthright daughter.'

Ella froze in the act of scanning the landscaped terraces for a waiter.

'Proud? Yes, yes, of course I am.' Her father

needed to improve his acting skills. He was usually an expert liar but Ella had never seen him so ill at ease. So desperate.

'And pretty too.'

Ella swung her head round to meet that probing gaze.

This had gone far enough. She'd done her best, rifling her sister's abandoned wardrobe to find something suitable. She wouldn't face a crowd of glittering socialites in work clothes and rubber-soled lace-up shoes. But she had no illusions. Fuzz was the one who turned heads. Never Ella.

'There's no need to butter me up. And I prefer not to be talked about as if I'm not here.'

'Ella!' Her father looked like he might have a stroke. His colour was too high and his pale eyes bulged before narrowing to needle-sharp fury. He really did need to change his lifestyle if he was going to make it into old age. As if he'd listen to her!

'My apologies, Ella.' That low velvety voice made her shiver. 'No insult was intended.'

'It's not you who should apologise, Donato.' Her father closed in, his grip biting her arm. 'I think—'

'*I* think,' Donato interrupted smoothly, 'it's time you left the pair of us to get better acquainted.'

For an instant her father stared. Usually he was smooth as oil, charming and quick with a comeback. Seeing him so patently at a loss was a new experience. Once it would have delighted Ella. Now a chill clamped her spine.

Who *was* this man with the power to frighten him so?

'Of course, of course.' Her father pasted on a toothy smile. 'You two need to get better acquainted. I'll let you do just that.' With one last warning pinch of her arm he released her and sauntered off as if he hadn't a care.

Ella watched him go. Ridiculously, she wanted to call him back. As if she hadn't spent most of her life avoiding him. As if he were the sort of father to protect her.

For the absolute conviction stiffening her sinews warned she really did need protection.

Abruptly she swung around, her gaze lifting until—there it was again—that jangle across her senses, that taut feeling of suspense as her gaze locked with Donato Salazar's.

His mouth tipped up in a smile that tugged at her heart, dragging it hard against her ribs, making it thrash like a landed fish. Her breath quickened as everything in her that was female responded to his ultra-male charisma.

Yet his eyes showed no softening. That stare probed her very being and found her wanting.

CHAPTER TWO

DONATO LOOKED DOWN into those clear eyes and felt the impact like the ripple of a stone plunging into deep, still water.

They weren't ordinary eyes. Oh, no, not Ms Ella Sanderson's. He'd yet to discover anything ordinary about her. He'd come here expecting her father's daughter and instead found…

What, exactly?

He didn't know yet but he intended to find out. He disliked being caught out.

Years ago, in prison, being caught off guard could have cost his life. It had almost cost him an eye. He'd made it his life's work to be in control, the one pulling the strings, never again reacting to forces he couldn't handle.

It had been a long time since anyone took him by surprise. He didn't like it.

Even though he liked what he saw. Too much.

Those eyes, for a start. Mercurial. Some indefinable shade between blue and grey that turned to silvery hoar frost when he riled her. He'd felt her disapproval like the jab from a shard of ice, straight to his belly.

Yet his overwhelming response was to wonder how her eyes would look when rapture overtook her. With him buried deep inside, feeling her shudder around him.

Was it any wonder he felt annoyed? She'd hijacked his thoughts, momentarily interfering with his plans.

She wasn't what he'd expected, or wanted. No man wanted that sudden sensation that he was no longer master of his destiny. That perfidious fate still had a few nasty surprises in store.

Fate be damned. Donato had stopped being its victim years ago.

'Alone at last,' he murmured, watching her mouth tighten.

So, she didn't like this thing sparking and snarling between them either. But as well as her caution and disapproval he sensed puzzlement. As if she didn't recognise the syrupy thickening of the atmosphere for what it was—carnal attraction.

Instant. Absolute. Undeniable.

'There's no need for us to be alone. Your business is with my father.' Her jaw angled belligerently.

Donato felt a quickening in his belly.

How long since a woman had reacted to him like that? Not with disdain because of his origins, but defiantly. The last few years had been littered with women eager to grab what they could—sex, money, status, even the thrill of being with a man with his dark reputation. How long since a woman he wanted had been difficult to attain?

For he found he wanted Ms Ella Sanderson with a primal hunger that would probably shock her. It disturbed him and he'd thought himself unshockable.

'But tonight is about socialising. This is a party, Ella.' He slowed on her name, enjoying the taste of it almost as much as he enjoyed the flicker of response in those bright eyes.

Oh, yes. Ms Sanderson wanted him as much as he did her. The way she swiped her lips with the tip of her tongue. The telltale tremble of the diamond drop earrings beside her slender throat. The way her eyelids drooped as if anticipating sexual pleasure. The quick rise of her lovely breasts against the azure satin of that tight dress.

Her nipples pebbled, thrusting towards him. It was all he could do not to reach out and anchor his palms against her breasts. He wanted their weight in his hands. He wanted more than he could take here, on one of the terraces leading down to the harbour from her father's mansion.

Donato shoved his hands into his trouser pockets and saw her eyes narrow to slits as if daring him to stare at her body.

'Do I disturb you, Ella?'

If she didn't want him to admire the view she should have worn something else, not a dress that clung to her curves like plastic wrap. In that at least she hadn't surprised him. He'd expected Sanderson's daughter to be like her father, show rather than substance. Till she'd turned to face him and he'd known with absolute certainty she was different.

'Of course not.' He liked her low, confident voice, so totally unlike the high-pitched giggles of the women by the pool, already shedding their inhibitions. 'Are you in the habit of...*disturbing* people?' Her tone wasn't arch with flirtation but serious, as if trying to fathom him.

That made two of them.

He shrugged, noting the way her gaze darted to his shoulders. Had he ever met a woman so primed and physically aware of him?

It made him want to take what he desired straight up, then worry about deciphering her later.

He took a step closer and she stilled. Even her breath seemed to stop. Her nostrils dilated. Did she breathe in his scent just as he found himself discovering she smelled of…sweet peas? The perfume of an old-fashioned garden.

Memory blindsided him. Of a garden in sunshine. Of his mother's all too rare laugh and Jack's patient tone as he taught them the difference between weeds and the precious vegetable seedlings.

How long since he'd thought of that?

It belonged in another lifetime.

'Donato?'

He stiffened, registering her hand, lifted as if reaching for him. Then it dropped to her side. He didn't know if he felt relief or regret.

He wanted to touch her, badly. But not here. Once they touched there would be no holding back.

'Some people find me disturbing.'

It would be comforting to believe he had this impact on everyone. Yet to Ella her response seemed utterly personal, as if something linked the pair of them.

'Why is that?'

Those jet eyebrows shot up. What? Surely not everyone was bowled over by those dark, fallen-angel looks? There must be some, heterosexual men and the blind, who were unaffected.

'What do you know about me?'

She shrugged. 'Just that my father wants to do business with you. Ergo you're rich and powerful.' She snapped her mouth shut before adding something uncomplimentary. She'd already shot her mouth off when she should have been smoothing the way for the news that her sister wouldn't be playing happy families.

It was remarkable how he'd provoked her into lashing out. Her profession required discretion.

'I know you're from Melbourne, visiting Sydney for a major project.'

'That's all?' His look penetrated, as if peering past the gloss of her sister's clothes and jewellery to the plain, no-frills woman beneath. Her traitorous body heated and she had to lock her knees.

'That's all.' She'd had no time for an Internet search. She'd barely had time after meeting her father to find suitable clothes to wear.

'You take so little interest in your father's business?'

'Yes.' She didn't elaborate. What her father did

was no longer any concern of hers. Except when it threatened Rob and Fuzz. 'That is—'

His raised hand silenced her. 'Don't explain. It's refreshing to meet someone honest enough to admit they're only interested in money, rather than how it's made.'

'You've got me wrong.' He made her sound like a leech.

'Have I? How?'

Belatedly she shook her head, caution stirring. 'Never mind. It's not relevant.'

They'd never meet again. It was a sign of weakness to worry about what he thought of her. Besides, she baulked at Donato Salazar knowing anything about her. Knowledge was power and he looked the sort to wield his power mercilessly.

'And what *is* relevant?'

'The reason you're here tonight. Felicity.'

'I came here expecting to meet her.' His gaze drifted over the crowd on the upper terraces.

'She's unavailable. She couldn't be here.'

'So your father mentioned.'

Ella wondered what else her father had said. She'd bet her whole savings account he hadn't admitted Fuzz had done a runner to north Queensland rather than face this man.

The idea of Fuzz anywhere without cold champagne on tap, working spa baths and an adoring audience was unbelievable. Yet Rob said they were camped in a couple of rooms at the old motel, making do with a primus stove and cold showers while the renovations were underway.

For the first time Fuzz was in love. Matthew, Rob's friend, now business partner, was decent, honest and hard-working, a rarity in her family's social circle. It gave Ella hope that Fuzz had fallen for him rather than the smarmy powerbrokers she'd dated before. Matthew's decision to turn the run-down motel he'd inherited into an upmarket resort had been the catalyst Rob and Fuzz needed to break from Sydney and their father.

'So you're standing in for your sister.' Donato's dark voice trawled like pure alcohol in Ella's veins, making her blood tingle. 'What could be more pleasant?'

His expression changed, lines deepening, gaze piercing. He looked…predatory.

Instantly heat bloomed.

'Not in the way you think!' Ella blurted.

'You know my thoughts?' Again that rise of slashing ebony eyebrows. It made him look like a haughty Spanish grandee of old.

'Of course not.' How did he throw her off balance so easily? She'd spent years learning to keep her thoughts to herself and her emotions under control. She always had both feet on the ground.

Yet around Donato Salazar she felt different.

He looked intent and assessing and his stare sent anxiety spidering across her flesh, drawing it tight. Ella wasn't used to such close masculine attention. Not from men like him. She felt out of her depth and that made her bristle. She decided to change the subject.

'I'm sure you'll enjoy yourself tonight. My father's parties are renowned.'

A shrill cry split the air, followed by a splash in the pool. There was laughter then another splash.

'So I gather.' His expression didn't change but there was steel in his tone that told her he had no time for party games. 'But I'm here to become acquainted with your family. With *you*, Ella.'

There it was again, that tremor of excitement as he said her name. Ella rubbed her hands up her bare arms to smooth sudden goose bumps. Too late she saw her mistake, when his gaze zeroed in on the movement. It wasn't cold. The night was balmy. He knew she was reacting to *him*.

Ella shouldn't have let pride tempt her into raiding her sister's wardrobe. Years as the frump of the family, the one with puppy fat and boring brown hair instead of glorious golden locks, had made her determined to look good. Now, wedged into her sister's dress, perched in glittery shoes, she craved her sensible trousers and flats.

She turned to lean on the waist-high terrace wall, pretending to look at the harbour view.

Donato stood over a metre away. Yet she *felt* him as if they touched. How was it possible?

'I didn't know until tonight that your father had three children. I'd only heard of two.'

That was no surprise. Reg Sanderson never boasted about his boring middle child as he did about his clever son or gorgeous older daughter. Until tonight Ella had been *persona non grata*.

'Felicity and Rob are closer to him. Rob even worked for him.' Until too-close exposure to their father's business soured his enthusiasm. Rob was a corporate lawyer and Ella suspected he'd seen too much of their father's business tactics.

'Yet I haven't seen photos of you with your sister in the press.'

Ella blinked. 'You read the social pages?' He looked the kind of man who only read finance and politics.

'You'd be surprised what I read.'

She frowned. 'It matters to you, does it? Who's seen at high-profile parties?'

'It matters that I understand people when I'm about to do business with them.'

Ella stiffened. 'Your business is with my father, not me or Felicity.'

His regard was enigmatic and unblinking. Challenging.

'You were checking up on her?'

He shrugged. 'Isn't it natural that I take an interest in your family?'

Since he planned to marry into it. Her stomach clenched.

'Did you hire investigators too?' She whipped around to face him full on.

'Why would that bother you?'

'Because it would be an invasion of privacy. It would be—' she shuddered '—intrusive.'

Had there been cameras trained on her sister when she partied? When she and Matthew were together? Ella frowned. Fuzz mightn't be the best sister in the world but she was the only one Ella had.

'Did you *spy* on my sister?' Ella stepped up to

Donato, her hands finding her hips, her bottom lip jutting.

'Your sister? No.' He was staring at her mouth.

Crazily, she felt her lips go dry. She swallowed and he watched the movement. How could it feel as if he trailed a finger down her throat when he hadn't lifted a hand?

Hormones. They danced riotously, making her heart drum against her ribcage and her insides clench needily.

Ella swiped her parched lips with her tongue and wished she hadn't. His look *seared*. She wanted to back up a step but he'd know why. She was stuck there, her neck arched to meet his intense scrutiny, her body taut as a spinnaker billowing and snapping in a sudden gale.

She didn't imagine the turbulence in the air. It was real and it emanated from *him*.

'You didn't hire investigators?' she pressed.

He shook his head, eyes never leaving hers. 'No one investigated you or your siblings. Otherwise I'd have known about you before tonight, wouldn't I?'

Ella drew in a deep breath, searching for calm. Trying to ignore the way her bra scraped her oversensitive breasts and budding nipples. Trying to concentrate on the conversation, not how this man made her feel.

It took a moment to realise what he *hadn't* said. He'd said nothing about whether he'd had her father investigated.

A sound made her turn. It was a waiter with a laden tray, coming down the stairs. Ella moved towards him. Her throat was dry but more, she craved something to distract her from the sensation of being cut off alone with Donato.

'Drink, sir? Ma'am?'

'Champagne, Ella?' Donato was right behind her. Had she really thought to escape so easily?

'Water, please.'

'Sensible choice.' He took two glasses of sparkling water and nodded his thanks to the waiter, who headed back to the higher terraces. Ella watched him go, wondering what would happen if she simply followed.

That wouldn't work. She needed to sort this out here, in private, away from curious eyes.

'Sensible?' Did he think she'd drink too much then lose her inhibitions?

Donato held out a drink, touching only the bottom of the glass, as if careful of any glancing contact.

Ella was inordinately grateful. Since they'd met

she'd felt his presence like a touch—on her lips, her skin, her breasts. She suspected the real thing—his skin against hers—might be her undoing.

Carefully she took the glass. 'Thanks.'

'Sometimes it's wise to keep a clear head. Tonight is one of those times.'

She'd lifted the glass to her lips but paused. Was he talking about her father's idea that he marry Fuzz? Or did he refer to the swirl of attraction enveloping them?

'About my father's proposal…'

'Which one?'

Ella stared. There was more than one?

Of course there was. The old man no doubt had a whole raft of business proposals for Donato. He'd be looking to screw every dollar he could out of him.

'About Felicity.'

'Yes?' Damn the man. He just stood there waiting, making her feel appallingly awkward.

Ella sipped her water, grateful for the cool fizz on her palate, easing the constriction in her throat. 'She's away long term. She has a commitment interstate.'

Donato nodded and Ella drew a relieved breath.

Of course he wasn't interested in her father's

suggestion that they marry. Donato Salazar would pick his own woman. He'd just been too polite to tell her father his idea was old-fashioned and unnecessary.

'She won't be coming back to Sydney.'

'So I understand.' He paused. 'Am I permitted to ask what keeps her away, or would that fall under the category of an invasion of privacy?'

Was he laughing at her?

'It's no secret. She's working in Queensland, managing a large interior-design project.'

'Really?' One eyebrow cocked up. 'I wasn't aware your sister actually worked.'

Ella felt a slow burn radiate out from her belly. Not sexual arousal this time but shame on Fuzz's behalf.

It was true. Her twenty-seven-year-old sister had never done a day's paid work. The closest she'd come were charity modelling gigs. But that was changing. Fuzz was committed to this project. If she stuck at it this would be the making of her. Once she was away from their father—

'As you say, Donato—' Ella halted, thrown for a second by how much she enjoyed saying his name. She was like a teenager stricken by lust for the first time! 'You don't know us.' She drew herself up, standing as tall as she could. 'Fuzz… Felicity is part of the design team for a major Queensland resort.' Well, it would be a major resort once it was finished.

'This is the resort your brother has invested in?'

'You know about that?'

'Your father said he'd left the family firm in order to strike out on his own. Still in the same field though, entertainment and hospitality.'

'Not quite the same. My father's wealth is built on gambling, poker machines and casinos.'

'Not just gambling.' The riposte came quickly and Ella tried to read that crisp tone. There was something adamantine in his voice, something new that sent anxiety skidding down her backbone. Instinct twanged in warning. She took another long sip of iced water, grounding herself.

'Your father has had diverse interests.' Ella thought she saw his lip curl. Then the impression was gone. He looked back blandly.

'Felicity has another reason for being in Queensland.' She needed to make it clear her father's scheme was impractical. 'She's living with her partner. They're working together.'

'A permanent relationship, then?'

'Absolutely.' More permanent, at least, than any of her sister's previous relationships. 'I know my father suggested you get to know Felicity better.' She couldn't bring herself to use the word *marry*. 'But in the circumstances that's not possible.'

'I understand completely.' Donato's lips curved in a smile that did the strangest things to her internal organs.

The man was devastating. Totally mind-blowingly gorgeous. He looked like some lethally enthralling anti-hero bent on breaking every rule, perhaps even ravishing a few virgins along the way.

Ella blinked and stared. What had got into her head? Flights of fancy were *so* not her.

Donato moved in, blocking her view of the other terraces and instantly her nerves jangled. She tightened her grip on the water glass, slippery with condensation.

'Your father thought our business partnership would be enhanced by a family tie. He suggested marriage.'

Ella waited for his derision at the idea. Instead she met only speculation in Donato's gaze.

'That's not an option. Felicity is spoken for,' she reiterated.

'I hope she'll be very happy.' Donato raised his glass in salute. 'And may I say how lucky I am that your father has another charming daughter to take her place?'

CHAPTER THREE

ELLA STARED INTO eyes that held not a whit of humour.

The hairs at her nape rose at the weight of that heavy-lidded regard.

Her, as her sister's replacement.

For a split second Ella felt triumph, elation at the prospect of being *his*. Of experiencing all that intensity, not as a curious specimen to be studied but as a lover.

Her gaze slewed to the breadth of those shoulders, the lean strength of the man beneath the exquisite tailoring. What would it feel like being held in those arms?

She reared back, water spilling from her glass.

'I'm not my sister's stand-in.' The words jerked out from her constricting throat.

'Of course not. You're a unique individual.' His smile was all smooth charm. If you didn't look into those eyes, calculating and *aware*.

'Don't patronise me.'

'My apologies. I assumed you'd prefer me to be frank.'

'Of course I do.' She gripped her glass in both hands.

He watched assessingly. 'Then let me say nothing appeals more than the prospect of knowing you better.'

There was nothing salacious in his tone, or his expression, yet those words—*knowing you*—held hidden depth. Knowing as in sexually knowing.

It should have horrified her yet it didn't.

She wanted him. Here. Now. With an immediacy that overrode every cautious, pragmatic, sensible bone in her body. With a raw hunger that totally disregarded the fact he was caviar and champagne in a crystal flute or perhaps arctic vodka, strong and lethal, while she was brown bread and tea in a good, sturdy pot.

'Don't be absurd. We have nothing in common.'

'I suspect we have a great deal in common, Ella.' He paused, as if savouring her name. 'Your father and his business, for instance.'

She spun away, stalking half a dozen steps before turning to face him. He was just as imposing, and smug, from here.

Then, to her dismay, he closed the gap with a couple of easy strides. Annoyance fizzed in her belly.

'You're not interested in getting to know *me*.' A man like Donato Salazar would want a high-profile trophy wife. Not a plain Jane woman whose feet ached at the end of a long day.

'I thought we'd already established that you don't know what goes on inside my head?'

He didn't look annoyed. Instead he looked…engaged. His tall body canted towards her as if drawn by the same force she felt urging her closer to him.

She stepped back, ignoring the knowing uptilt of those slashing eyebrows.

She understood attraction. Even understood the lure of the dangerous, though she'd always chosen a safer, more prosaic route through life.

Yet she'd never experienced this heat of desire. It saturated her, made her imagine impossible things. Like grabbing Donato's collar and yanking that proud, scarred face down to hers. She wanted to savour him, lose herself in the passion she knew was hiding below that veneer of polite calm.

His nostrils flared, his chest rising sharp and sudden, as if he'd intercepted her thoughts. His gaze dropped to her mouth.

The night air zapped and thickened.

'I don't know anything about you.'

'But that doesn't matter, does it?' His deep voice wove around her. 'It doesn't stop what you're feeling.'

Ella opened her mouth to snap that she felt *nothing.*

But he was watching keenly, waiting for her to flutter and fuss and deny this *awareness* between them. She wouldn't play coy. It would be an admission of fear and showing fear to this man would only invite trouble.

Ella jerked her chin up. 'I don't know what sort of women you usually mix with, Donato. But know this. I'm not about to act on impulse with a stranger.'

'No matter how tempting.' He gave voice to her thoughts, making her start.

'What?' he drawled, his voice like honey and gravel. 'You think I'm not tempted? You think my hands aren't itching to slide over your luscious body? To pull you tight against me and feel how well we fit? To taste you?'

The sudden change from amused outsider to consummate seducer slammed her heart against her ribs.

'You think I'm not tempted to make you acknowledge exactly how much you want me?'

Ella's breath disintegrated. His gaze flickered to her heaving breasts and fire exploded within. She was burning up and nothing, she suspected, could put out the conflagration except Donato.

The idea appalled as much as it excited her.

She looked at the glass shaking in her too-tight grip. Had her drink been spiked? How she wished she had such an easy excuse.

'It doesn't matter what you want, Donato.' She lifted her head to meet his stare. 'It's not going to happen.'

His gaze sharpened and anxiety feathered through her. Too late she pondered the wisdom of declaring an outright challenge. She had a disturbing feeling Donato Salazar thrived on smashing challenges.

'Never say never, Ella.'

The intensity of his look scared her. Suddenly she felt out of her depth. She wanted to be in her flat, curled up in her pyjamas with a movie and the block of chocolate she'd been saving all week.

'I want to know you, Ella.'

'How? Sexually?' She put her glass down on a nearby table before she dropped it.

'I like that you say exactly what you think, Ella. It's refreshing.'

She stuck her hands on her hips and this time she did give in to impulse, stalking a step closer till she realised her mistake and shuddered to a halt. But she refused to backtrack, even though she stood near enough to inhale his heady masculine scent.

'You're a slow learner, Donato. I told you not to patronise me.'

He shook his head. 'I'm just telling you the truth.' His mouth widened in a smile that drew her belly tight. 'Do I want your body? Absolutely.' His gaze dipped then rose again. 'We'll be magnificent together.'

No *if*, just absolute certainty. Where did this man get off, assuming she was his for the taking?

'But I want more. I want to understand you.'

Of all the things he could have said, of all the things he *had* said, this was the one that cut her defences off at the knees.

No man had ever wanted to understand her. Not her father, who'd wanted her to be pretty and frivolous and pander to his ego. Not the guys she'd met at long-ago society parties, nor the men she'd dated since.

Longing coursed through her. He was clever, this man, too clever. He really did know what women wanted.

'Why?' She tilted her head to one side, wishing she could read him. 'We're strangers. And don't tell me it's because you think my father's idea of marrying into this family is a good one. I want the truth.'

Ella held herself tall, ready for Donato's blast of outrage, conditioned to it after a lifetime dealing with her father's volatile temperament.

'You think I'd lie?'

'Men usually do when they want something.'

'You don't have a high opinion of men.' He looked curious rather than offended. 'But I applaud your caution.'

'You do?'

He nodded. 'It pays not to accept everything at face value. Too many people put themselves at risk then find themselves in situations they can't control or escape.' His voice rang with a depth of feeling that surprised her.

She couldn't imagine anyone taking advantage of Donato.

'Did that ever happen to you?'

Long moments passed, then he surprised her.

'Of course. But once was enough. It won't happen again.' His words held absolute certainty.

Ella wished she possessed such conviction. She should walk away from Donato Salazar and the danger he represented. He made her want things that scared the daylights out of her.

She imagined giving in to him. There'd be no fumbling, no awkwardness. She guessed with him sex would be far too easy and utterly devastating.

'Why me?' She set her jaw. 'There are plenty of glamorous women here. Quite a few would give you sex if you asked.'

'You don't think you're glamorous?'

How had he latched onto that? On the fact she felt like an imposter even dressed in silk and diamonds.

'I know my limitations.'

'And you think your looks are one of them?'

'The way I look doesn't matter.' She ignored the tension clamping her stomach.

He put down his drink beside hers and she wondered, frantically, if he'd reach for her. Instead he shoved his hands into his trouser pockets. The movement emphasised the power in both his broad shoulders and muscular thighs.

'I think it matters very much, *to you*.'

Ella wiped clammy hands down her dress. Her sister's dress. Fuzz would look delicate and gorgeous in it. On Ella it strained at the seams and the skirt rode too high.

'I was wrong when I called you pretty.'

She froze. She'd asked for the truth, hadn't she? What did it matter if these last few years she'd begun to believe she was attractive in her own quiet way? His admission shouldn't feel like such a blow.

'Pretty is for little girls. And you're all woman, Ella.' She saw his hands bunch in his pockets, drawing the fabric of his trousers tight. 'You're the only woman here that I want in my bed.'

Her breath was an audible gasp.

'You're stunning. The fire in your eyes, that sassy mouth of yours, all that lovely lush bounty of hips and breasts and long, long legs. I want—'

'That's enough!'

Ella pressed a palm to her pounding chest. Her heart hammered up high as if it had broken free. 'We're not discussing my looks or who you want in your bed.'

'We're not?' His mouth kicked up at the corner in a tiny smile that was far more devastating than the one he'd given her before. It was the sort of smile a friend or lover might give, a shared intimacy.

Ella tugged the silk dress further down her thighs. 'No. We're discussing the fact that you marrying into the Sanderson family is totally unnecessary.'

'Unnecessary? Yes.'

At last! She felt as if a huge stone lifted off her chest. Finally some of the tension drained from her body.

'But definitely appealing.' His eyes traced a sinuous line down her tall frame and it was a wonder Ella didn't self-combust. If any other man had ogled her like that she'd have slapped him. Instead her shoulders tightened, pushing out her breasts as if she revelled in that proprietorial look.

'I beg your pardon?' Pity the words sounded breathy rather than outraged.

'You heard me, Ella. Don't play coy.'

'I'm not playing anything!' Had the world gone mad? Had lust addled her brain? 'You can't seriously tell me you think my father's plan makes sense.'

'Actually—' his eyes locked with hers '—I think it's an excellent idea.'

'You've got to be kidding.' She stared into that

steady blue gaze, waiting for some sign that Donato was joking.

No sign came. Ella folded her hands over her chest then wished she hadn't when his gaze flickered to her breasts, pushed up under the tight silk. She hated how that split-second glance flustered her.

'It's not going to happen. Felicity won't marry you.'

'So you said.' He leaned forward, holding her gaze. 'You're repeating yourself. Do I make you nervous?'

'Nervous? No.' Casually she reached for her discarded glass and took a slow sip.

'Something else then?' His voice was a dark purr. Instead of reassuring, it primed her fight-or-flight response. Donato was no tame cat. He was about as safe as a panther eyeing its next meal.

'Several things spring to mind, Donato, but I'm too polite to spell them out.'

His chuckle was warm treacle spilling through her veins. 'It's been an absolute pleasure meeting you tonight, Ella. I hadn't expected to enjoy myself so much.'

'I amuse you?' Her jaw firmed, her look dared him to laugh at her.

'That's not the word I'd use.' Abruptly his laughter died. His expression was sombre and intent.

'I don't want to know.'

His eyebrows arched. 'You don't? I hadn't pegged you for a coward, Ella.'

She shook her head. 'I'm not afraid of you.' She was too busy being terrified of the stranger she'd become while she was with him.

'Good, that will make things so much more enjoyable.'

'What things?'

He rocked back on his heels. 'Our relationship.'

'We don't *have* a relationship. I'm going to leave and you'll spend the rest of the evening enjoying the party.' It was a test of willpower not to look at the pool terrace, where the laughter had escalated to riotous. He'd be welcomed with open arms. 'We won't see each other again.'

The realisation was like a rock plummeting inside her stomach. Despite all tonight's negatives, Ella felt invigorated, more energised than she had in ages.

'Why? Do you have a man waiting up for you?' Donato dragged his hands out of his pockets, his stance widening as he folded his arms across his chest. The movement transformed him from lazy spectator to belligerent adversary. Or maybe it was the way he scowled.

'There's no one waiting up for me.' Ella could have bitten her tongue. He brought out the reckless, unthinking side she usually managed to squash.

'Excellent. I won't be stepping on anyone's toes.'

Ella read his smug expression and her fingers slipped on the damp glass. There was a crash. Water sprayed her bare leg as the glass shattered on the flagstones.

'Are you okay?' He stepped forward, so close he stole her air. His hand lifted as if to touch her and something engulfed her—a warmth, a frisson, an unseen shimmer of electrical charge.

'Fine! I'm fine.' Ella assumed it was water trickling down her calf, not blood from a tiny cut. She'd look later.

She stepped back, coming up against the stone wall. She swallowed down panic. 'It's been a very long day and I'm tired.' With an effort she kept her words even. 'Find someone else to play your games.'

Piercing eyes scrutinised her, then Donato nodded and stepped aside to let her pass. Relief stirred.

'You underestimate me, Ella. I'm not playing games. I'll call for you in the morning.'

'Why? There's no point.'

There was no smile on his features when he answered. 'To get to know you before the wedding, of course.'

'Cut it out, Donato. The joke's over.' Was that a wobble in her voice? Great. Just great. Ella stalked past.

To her horror he turned, his long stride fitting to hers, his hand hovering at the small of her back. She *felt* it as surely as if he'd pressed his palm to her spine.

'I'll walk you to the house.'

'I can get there alone.'

'You're tired. I'll keep you company.'

Ella slammed to a halt and a whisper of sensation glanced down her back as his hand skimmed her dress. An instant later he'd stepped back.

It was more than tiredness bothering her. Being back in her father's house, she had that awful sensation she'd known in her teens, that she was dressing up, pretending to be someone she wasn't. She'd even grown klutzy again, though she worked with her hands all the time.

Worse, being watched by Donato unnerved her. As for his pretence that he wanted to marry her!

That made her burn from the soles of her feet to the tips of her ears.

'Now you listen!' She swung around and lifted a hand to jab her index finger into that imposing chest.

To her surprise Donato stepped back before she made contact.

'Don't.' The single word was terse. His face hardened, grew still but for the tic of a pulse at his temple.

'What?' He didn't like her invading his personal space? Tough. She didn't like being the butt of his joke. She planted her hands on her hips and moved even closer.

'Not a good idea, Ella.'

'Why not? You can dish it out but you can't cope with a woman who stands up to your cruel little games?' Silly to taste disappointment. For a while there she'd almost believed there was more to Donato.

That proved it. She *was* tired.

His lips thinned, curling up in a smile unlike either of the ones she'd seen before. This one held no warmth or humour. It was a hunter's assessing look and it was full of satisfaction. It brought her up sharply, her heart thrumming frantically.

'On the contrary, Ella.' His voice slowed to syrup on her name. 'I can't tell you how much I'm looking forward to you *standing up against me*.'

Dazed, Ella wondered if he too pictured them locked together, she held high in his embrace, her legs around his waist. She swallowed, willing the fiery blush away.

Then she read the tension in his neck and shoulders, in his clenched hands. 'Don't try to con me, Donato. You don't like me being this close to you.'

'Brave but foolish, Ella.' He unfurled his hands, stretching his long fingers, and abruptly Ella felt far too close for comfort. 'I don't want you *near* me. I want you *against* me, skin to skin, with nothing between us. I want to watch you blush, not just with arousal—' his gaze trawled her heated face '—but with ecstasy.'

Her gasp was loud in the throbbing silence.

He breathed deep, his chest rising so high Ella could swear she felt a disturbance in the air, brushing her breasts and drawing her nipples to tight buds. Her body blazed with the fire he'd ignited.

'I drew back,' he murmured, 'because when we *do* touch, I want us to be alone. So we can finish what we start.' His eyes were heavy-lidded yet there was nothing lazy about his scrutiny. She felt it in the jangle of her nerves. That only made her angrier.

'You expect me to believe one touch from me and you wouldn't be able to control yourself?' Her eyebrows arched. She wasn't that naïve, despite the foolish way her body responded. She was no siren, to make men forget themselves.

'I know neither of us would want to pull back once we…connected.' He let his words sink in. 'I also suspect your desire for privacy might be even stronger than mine. Anyone could walk down here and interrupt us.'

He looked around as if searching for a suitable spot for them to get naked together.

'I don't believe you.'

His gaze collided with hers. 'You want to test it?' His nostrils flared, his eyes gleaming slits. He looked primitive, dangerous, like a warrior daring her to combat.

Her brain screamed a warning and Ella stepped back. The scrape of her heel on the flagstone was unnaturally loud. Even her breathing was amplified, and her pulse, beating that quick tattoo.

'No, I don't want to touch you. Not now, not ever.' Just as well there was no summer thunderstorm tonight or she might have been struck down for the enormity of that lie. 'I won't be seeing you again, Donato. Goodbye.'

Squaring her shoulders, half expecting him to stop her, Ella turned and strode along the terrace back towards the bright lights and people.

He let her go. See, it had been easy after all. She'd called Donato's bluff and that was the end of it.

That was *not* disappointment she felt. It was relief that she'd never have to see him again.

CHAPTER FOUR

DONATO WATCHED ELLA march away. He'd thought nothing about Reg Sanderson could surprise him. Yet Sanderson's daughter had stopped him in his tracks.

Ella. He savoured her name.

Perhaps it had been a mistake pulling away from her. Maybe if he hadn't kept his distance he'd have shattered this illusion that she was different.

Except it would take more than a quickie up against the garden wall to quench what was inside him.

Which, he assured himself, fitted his plans perfectly.

That was what he had to concentrate on. Revenge. He'd always known it would be sweet. With Ella as an added bonus it would be delicious.

He sauntered to the house. There was no one here he wanted to spend time with. Only Ella. Despite her bravado he'd read her fear. Sensible woman. But he'd allay those fears and ensure she enjoyed their time together.

He'd stopped to tell a waiter about the broken glass on the lower level when Sanderson appeared. His pale eyes looked almost febrile, belying his casual stance. Satisfaction stirred. This had been a long time coming. Too long. He intended to enjoy every moment of Sanderson's descent into ruin.

'All alone, Donato?' He scowled. 'Where's that girl of mine? Don't tell me she's left you alone?'

'Ella was tired.'

'Tired? I'll give her tired!' he roared. 'I—'

'It's better she gets her sleep tonight.' Donato kept his voice bland though he wanted to grab Sanderson by the scruff of his neck and shake him till his teeth rattled.

Because Donato hated him with every fibre of his being? Or because of the way he spoke of Ella? Didn't the man realise how precious family was? Had he no concept of protecting his child against a man whom everyone knew was as implacable and dangerous as they came?

What sort of man sold his daughter to a stranger?

Donato already knew the answer. Reg Sanderson. The bastard had already destroyed too many lives.

It would be a public service as well as a pleasure to see he got his just deserts.

Darkness engulfed him. No, Donato wouldn't see him dead, which was what he deserved. Donato had come close to killing once and he'd learned a lot since then. This way was better. Sanderson's suffering would be drawn out.

'She should have stayed here, with you. I apologise.'

Donato raised his hand. 'It doesn't matter. I'll see her tomorrow.'

'You will?' The older man's expression stilled. 'So, you're interested? In *Ella*?' Was that barely concealed shock in his voice? Sanderson had no notion what a gem his daughter was. The man was blind as well as deplorable.

Donato had seen the photos of Ella's sister, a golden girl with obvious allure. Yet if he really sought a bride he wouldn't choose Felicity Sanderson. If reports were accurate, she hadn't a loyal bone in her body.

Did Ella really believe her sister would stick with this new lover, or did she merely try to protect her from the danger he, Donato, represented?

The idea of her protecting anyone from him was ludicrous, given his far superior power and resources. Yet the notion stuck and he filed it away for future consideration.

'It was a delight meeting someone so refreshing and intelligent.' Forthright and clever enough to be suspicious, Ella had intrigued from the instant she'd looked at him.

Sanderson didn't quite hide his satisfaction. His smile was hungry. 'It's wonderful you hit it off so well. I'd hoped you would. There's no telling with Ella; sometimes she can be a little…'

'A little…?'

Sanderson shrugged and took a swig of his drink. 'To be frank, she can be a little outspoken sometimes. But in a good way, of course. Refreshing, as you say.'

He smiled that conspiratorial smile as if they were good buddies and Donato had to repress the compulsion to slam his fist into the other man's whiter than white capped teeth. He'd done a lot of things in his time, some of them society had labelled reprehensible. But nothing that sickened him like playing Sanderson's temporary friend.

'I prefer honesty to polite platitudes.' Especially when those platitudes hid murky secrets.

'Don't we all?'

'Meeting your daughter has helped me feel I

know you better. That's important if we're to work together.'

'I thought you'd see it that way.' Sanderson paused, then said carefully, 'So, you want to proceed with the partnership and the loan?' His absolute stillness gave him away. He was strung tight.

Grim satisfaction filled Donato. 'Definitely. This is too good an opportunity to miss.'

It had taken years of preparation to reach this point, and now he was poised to destroy Sanderson financially and socially. If he couldn't put him behind bars for his crimes, Donato would at least see he lost what he cared for most. 'My staff are ready to meet at ten tomorrow to discuss the details.'

'You won't be there?' Concern flared in Sanderson's eyes. Excellent. It was time he discovered he couldn't keep running from the consequences of his actions.

'My staff are competent to handle the meeting. I plan to be with Ella, getting to know her better.'

'I'm sure she'll love that.'

Not initially, Donato knew, but he'd change her mind. He looked forward to it.

'Does that mean you liked my notion of a Salazar-Sanderson marriage?' Sanderson looked urbane and relaxed, yet the ripple on the surface of his whisky betrayed him.

Donato scrutinised him, from his deep tan and perennially gold hair to the gloss only close acquaintance with serious money could buy. That didn't hide the mean lines around his mouth, the avaricious gleam in those pale blue eyes or the pugnacious angle of that thick jaw.

He knew what Sanderson was. Imagine him as a father. No wonder his eldest daughter was a beautiful waste of space. Which made his younger daughter…what, exactly?

'Donato?' Sanderson didn't sound quite so smug now.

'The marriage idea?' Donato took his time, relishing the other man's unease. 'I think it's an excellent one.'

Sanderson's eyes widened momentarily before his face eased into a calculating look. 'Ella is a special girl, and lucky.' His toothy smile reminded Donato of a crocodile. Or maybe it was just that he knew Sanderson to be as cold-blooded as any reptile.

Despite the money he'd made, Donato had no illusions that he was love's young dream. Not with his criminal record. He was the sort of man parents prayed their daughter would never bring home.

Yet here was Sanderson thrusting his unsuspecting daughter into Donato's arms. Was there anything Sanderson wouldn't do for money?

'And Ella agreed?' Pale eyes fixed on him.

'Ella understands what I want. We'll sort out the details soon.'

'It will be a pleasure welcoming you to the family.' Sanderson made to shake hands but Donato pretended not to notice, turning to snag a wine glass from a passing waiter.

'Here's to the wedding that will make us family.' Sanderson raised his glass.

Donato suppressed a wave of nausea at the notion of being so intimately linked with this man. Sanderson had destroyed the one person Donato had ever loved. The only one who'd ever loved him. Sanderson had destroyed countless others too and didn't give a damn. But Donato did, and he'd make sure Sanderson paid in full.

'To the wedding,' he murmured. 'Soon, don't you think?'

'Definitely.' Sanderson nodded. 'Though Ella might—'

'I'm sure I can persuade her to an early date.'

The thought of persuading Ella made his blood hum. He was counting the hours till he saw her again. That was a first.

His host nodded. 'I knew you'd be the man for her. A lovely girl, but she needs a firm hand.'

Was that how Sanderson had managed his family? Donato's investigators had concentrated on Sanderson's business activities, especially any nasty little financial secrets, not on his family. Sympathy flickered, even for party girl Felicity. But most of all for Ella. Ella, with the wary eyes, who didn't believe she was beautiful.

'Don't worry. You can leave Ella to me.'

'Good man.' Sanderson waved his whisky glass. 'I suppose you'd prefer to marry in Melbourne so I suggest—'

'No, I couldn't do that. I know the bride's family organises the wedding. You'll want to give Ella a big society event.' Donato smiled, genuine amusement surfacing at Sanderson's dismay. Obviously, in his scheming to snare Donato's support, and money, he hadn't reckoned with footing the bill for a lavish celebration.

'That's kind, Donato. But you're a very private man. Ella will understand if you want to tie the knot quietly.'

Donato shook his head. 'I wouldn't dream of depriving her. The bigger the celebration the better. It will signal the beginning of our partnership.' There, that made him smile. 'Let's make it the society event of the decade.'

Donato watched his host turn a pasty shade of green. 'I realise it's a huge task organising such an event at short notice so I'll give you some assistance.'

'That's very good of you, Donato. I won't say no.'

'Good. I'll lend you someone to help with the preparations. I know just the person. She's got an eye for quality and understands we'll want no expense spared.' He put up his hand when Sanderson would have interrupted. 'Don't thank me. It's the least I can do.'

Sanderson bit back a response, his expression for a moment ugly, though quickly masked.

'Now, if you'll just give me Ella's mobile number? I forgot to get it earlier.'

Interestingly, for a man who thought his daughter so 'special', Sanderson didn't have the number programmed into his phone. He had to go inside to get it, leaving Donato to consider the outcome of tonight's events.

Sanderson was on the hook.

As for his absurd proposal that Donato marry his daughter…that was the bid of a desperate man.

But Donato would play along. It would be the icing on the cake to know his enemy had spent his last credit on a huge public wedding that would never take place. Not only would Sanderson be ruined beyond redemption, the farce of the non-wedding would make him a social pariah.

Even if Donato had to come in quietly later and pay the bills so no suppliers were out of pocket, the expense would be worth it. Sanderson would be in the gutter, ashamed and ostracised, bankrupt and unable to start again. He deserved far worse but it would do.

Only one thing niggled. When Sanderson had first suggested marriage, Donato had had no qualms about agreeing. From what he'd learned, Felicity had a Teflon-coated heart. She'd thrive on the notoriety and the monetary compensation Donato would provide when the wedding was cancelled.

But Ella was different. He didn't yet have her measure and that gave him pause. He never went into negotiations without knowing his opponent. Or in this case his partner.

His lips tilted in a satisfied smile. No, it didn't

matter if this once he winged it. He'd work out a way to compensate her. But he had no intention of walking away. Not merely because this dovetailed so nicely with his plans for revenge. But because he wanted Ella.

He intended to enjoy her, and their courtship, to the full.

CHAPTER FIVE

''LO...?' ELLA DRAGGED the phone to her ear, burrowing deeper into her bed. It was far too early on a Saturday morning for anyone to call.

'Not a morning person, Ella?' The deep voice poured through the phone to ripple like soft suede over her bare skin. Instantly she was alert, her eyes popping open to survey the morning light sneaking around the edges of her bedroom curtains.

'Who is this?' Her voice sounded prim, almost schoolmarmish, but it was her best effort. She'd gone to sleep with the sound of Donato's voice in her ears; she'd even dreamt of it when she eventually managed to snatch some sleep. It was unfair to be confronted with it now when she hadn't had time to gather herself.

'As if you don't know, sweet Ella. Did I wake you?' The words worked like a caress, drawing her skin taut, jerking her free of the last traces of sleep. That voice should be outlawed. It was too decadent, too delicious to be unleashed on an unsuspecting woman.

'Yes. No!' She rolled her eyes in frustration. 'Who's speaking?'

'Forgotten your fiancé already?' His voice plumbed new depths, curling heat right down inside her. 'I can see I'll have to try harder.'

'Donato.' No point pretending. 'What do you want?' She wouldn't dignify that fiancé joke with a response.

'I told you last night want I wanted.'

Her. That was what he'd said. And her body had gone into libido overdrive at the look in his sultry eyes.

'But for now just tell me, are you still in bed?'

'What if I am?' Ella frowned. Why? Was he somewhere nearby? Had her father given him her address? Surely not. Donato Salazar wouldn't venture into the working-class suburbs in search of her. Though, after what she'd learned about him on the Web when she got home, he wasn't a stranger to poor neighbourhoods. She still found it hard to believe what she'd discovered.

'Tell me what you're wearing.' The words raked her skin, drawing it tight over a belly that clenched needily.

Just at the sound of his voice?

Ella bit back a moan. This couldn't be happening to her.

'Tell me, Ella. Pyjamas?' He paused. 'A nightie?' Another pause, longer this time. 'Silk and lace?'

She firmed her lips, not letting herself rise to the bait.

'Or do you sleep naked?'

The gasp escaped her lips before she could stop it. Weirdly, it felt as if, just by saying it, he must know.

And now he did. She'd given herself away with that intake of breath. She heard it in his voice. 'Give me your address and I'll be straight over.'

'No!' Her voice hit top register. Her heart was pounding as she heard his dark-chocolate chuckle against her ear.

She wanted to tell him she didn't usually sleep naked. It had just been so hot last night and she couldn't get comfortable, even after a cold shower. But she knew he'd put two and two together and realise it wasn't the summer heat that had kept her from sleep, but thoughts of him. His ego was big enough already.

'Why are you ringing, Donato?'

'It's not enough that I want to hear your voice?'

That sounded like a parody of her own feelings. She tried to despise this man who was a crony of her father's, who'd toyed with her last night. Yet she kept the phone pressed to her ear, luxuriating in the soft rumble of his voice. As if she *wanted* that flurry of desire rippling through her.

Ella shuffled up in the bed, yanking the pillows up behind her so she could sit. Lying naked in bed with Donato's voice in her ear was wrong on so many levels.

'Get to the point, Donato. Why did you call?'

'Do you usually sleep so late?'

Ella peered at the time, stunned to find it was after nine. 'No.' Usually she was up at six to fit in Pilates or a swim before work.

'So you had a disturbed night? Were you dreaming about me?' That thread of satisfaction in his voice grew stronger.

'Is there a point to this call?' She sighed ostentatiously as if she hadn't indeed spent half the night taunted by dreams of him. 'Or do I hang up now?'

'Give me your address so I can collect you. We're having lunch together.'

Ella scowled. She told herself it was because of his assumption she'd go along with what he wanted. But what unnerved her was the little jiggle of excitement that skipped through her.

'Ella?'

'If you'd invited me to lunch I'd be obliged to thank you for the invitation before I declined. But as there was no invitation that's unnecessary.'

'Absolutely,' he said smoothly. 'Because we *will* be lunching together.'

Ella shifted against the pillows. She shouldn't enjoy this fruitless argument. Yet she couldn't bring herself to end the call. Not when basking in the sound of Donato's voice was the closest she'd come to enjoying a man's company in a long, long time.

What did that say about the state of her love life?

Pathetic! That was it.

'What's your address, Ella?'

'I'm surprised a man with your resources doesn't already have it.' Her father would have given it to him in an instant, if he'd been able to find it. 'Don't tell me your dossier on the Sanderson family doesn't include something so basic.'

'I don't have a dossier on your family.'

'I thought you'd be a better liar, Donato.'

Instead of taking offence he chuckled again, the sound like warm water lapping through her veins.

Ella's hand on the phone grew clammy and her bare nipples budded. Frowning, she snatched the sheet and dragged it up, anchoring it under her arms. As if that would protect her from whatever this magic was he wove around her.

'I have a dossier on your father's business and on his private…interests.' Ella winced, not liking the sound of that. There were some things she didn't need to know about her father. 'And some information on your sister.'

'You told me you didn't set your investigators onto her!'

'I didn't need to. A quick trawl through the social pages was more than ample.'

Ella hated the way he dismissed Fuzz as if she were nothing. Her sister might be flawed but she wasn't as bad as all that. She just needed purpose, and freedom from their father's influence.

'Really?' Her voice dripped disapproval.

'It seemed a sensible precaution since your father suggested I marry her.'

And now Fuzz was out of the picture that left Ella.

Ella glanced around the bedroom with its Monet print on the wall and her pride and joy, the nineteen-twenties tub chair she'd rescued from a garage sale and reconditioned with the help of a night class. The wooden legs glowed with polish and the sage-green upholstery was restful as well as pretty.

The idea of strangers nosing into her world, ordinary as it was, picking through the details of her life, set her teeth on edge.

'I don't make it into the social pages. How much have you found out about me?'

'Not nearly enough.' The skin at Ella's nape drew tight at the sultry note in that deep voice.

'Your investigators only work business hours? You disappoint me, Donato. I'd have thought they'd scurry to do the bidding of a man with your reputation even late last night.'

'You've been doing some digging of your own.' He didn't sound fazed.

'Don't tell me you're offended?'

'On the contrary, I'm pleased. It proves that, despite your rather emphatic goodbye, you anticipated meeting me again.'

Ella scowled. He was right. Why bother finding out about him if she'd cut him from her life? She'd had an insidious certainty it wasn't so easy to get rid of Donato Salazar.

No, it was more than that. She'd wanted to know

everything she could about him. No man had ever made such an impact on her.

'And as for hiring investigators to work through the night…'

'Yes?' She shifted uneasily. Was someone even now interviewing her neighbours or accessing her records?

'You made it clear you believed that an unforgivable breach of privacy.'

'So?'

'So I'm not going to do it to you.'

'Sorry?'

'You heard me, Ella. I'm not in the habit of saying things I don't mean.'

For a moment words eluded her. 'Just like that? Because I said so?'

'Just like that.'

Ella's pulse faltered then tripped to an unfamiliar beat. He was serious. Yet she couldn't quite believe he'd renege on using the power his money could buy just because it offended her.

Why would he do that?

She shoved her hair back from her face. To her amazement her fingers were ever so slightly unsteady.

What did he want from her?

Surely he'd been lying last night, saying he wanted to know her. As for that nonsense about them marrying—

'I want to know everything about you.' His deep voice burred in her ear. 'But I want to find out from you.'

She'd known Donato Salazar was dangerous, but still she wasn't prepared for the way he devastated her defences. It took precious seconds to find her voice. 'I'm afraid you're going to be disappointed.'

'Nothing about you is disappointing, believe me, *Ella*.' There it was again, that caress when he said her name. As if those two simple syllables were an endearment.

'I meant—' she set her jaw '—you'll be disappointed because we're not going to meet again.'

He was silent and stupidly something like anxiety feathered through her. At the idea this was the last time she'd speak with him? Impossible!

'Are you scared of me, Ella?'

'Scared? No.' Strangely enough, it was true. She was scared of what he made her feel, of the urgent, restless woman she'd become in the short time since they'd met. But not scared of him.

'Not even after what you discovered in your

research on me?' The banter was gone from his voice. He sounded deadly serious.

Deadly. Now there was a word. Last night she'd thought he looked dangerous. Then, at home, sitting with her computer, she'd discovered how right she'd been. How many people had she known personally who'd been to prison for assault?

None.

Was it naïve of her to believe that, despite his teenage criminal record, Donato Salazar wouldn't hurt her?

She'd been stunned to read about his crime and his prison term. At the same time it went some way to explaining the sense she'd had last night that he was a man apart from everyone else.

As a nurse she'd worked with a huge range of people, from the frail aged to the bloodied survivors of brawls to the drug-addicted and downright dangerous. She was cautious, methodical, never taking unnecessary risks, especially doing home visits. But the only alarm she felt now was at her own avid response to Donato.

'I'm not afraid of you because you've got a criminal record, Donato.' In the intervening years he'd built a reputation for ruthlessness in business but there'd never been a hint he was anything but a model citizen. He'd been lauded for his work supporting inner-city youth centres and legislation to assist victims of abuse.

'Then you're unique.' Was that bitterness she heard? She hitched herself higher against the pillows.

'Are you saying I should be? That you're violent?'

'No.' His voice was flat. 'I'm not that person any more. I've learned to restrain my impulses. Instead I channel them into something more productive.'

He said nothing for a moment and she wondered what was going through his mind. 'So, you're not frightened. But you *are* curious.'

'You're not the average Australian business tycoon.'

His laugh was sharp but appealing and despite herself Ella's lips twitched. How could she feel at ease with this man? His past and his dealings with her father should warn her off, yet she felt incredibly drawn to him. It wasn't just desire; she was fascinated by the way his mind worked. She enjoyed their verbal sparring.

'You've met lots of tycoons, have you?'

'A few.'

'And you weren't impressed.'

By the men with whom her father did business? 'Not usually.'

'But still you want to know me better. Here's the chance to satisfy your curiosity, Ella. Over lunch. We have a table reserved at the Opera House restaurant. I'm assured the food is excellent.'

But it wasn't food on his mind, or even conversation. The low pitch of his voice was pure seduction. Ella pressed her thighs together, pretending she didn't feel that tiny pulse of awareness awakening between them.

'No, thank you.'

There was a pause. 'Has anyone ever told you you're stubborn?'

'Yes.'

'You know you want to. You're denying yourself as well as me.'

'Don't presume to know my mind, Donato.'

He sighed. 'Don't make me force you, Ella.'

She tucked the sheet more securely under her arms and sat straighter. 'You can't force me.'

'What if I told you your father's financial viability is totally dependent on my support? And that support is dependent on the wedding he's organising for us.'

'You're lying. You don't want to marry me. We discussed it last night.'

What sort of bizarre game was he playing?

'*You* discussed it, Ella, but you wouldn't listen to my response.' He paused and the silence thickened around her. 'Ask your father if you don't believe me. He'll confirm it. The wedding goes ahead or there's no deal. And if there's no deal…'

CHAPTER SIX

DONATO WAS WAITING for her, standing in the doorway of a white, two-storey art deco gem of a mansion that made Ella's mouth water with envy. In the forecourt sat a gleaming convertible in dark red. Not a modern supercar but a vintage model with running boards that made her think of champagne picnics and romantic escapes to the country.

She choked down annoyance. It was easier to loathe the man before she realised they shared the same tastes.

But this wasn't his home. Donato lived in Melbourne. Maybe he was a guest here. He probably lived in a soulless box of a house and had a chauffeur drive him in a stretch limo.

The thought soothed her. She didn't like the notion they had anything in common. Anything other than that disconcerting stir of attraction. And the suspicion she'd got last night that he wasn't a fan of her father. Clearly that was pure imagination, since he proposed to link himself with Reg Sanderson's family.

Ella stopped her little car, telling herself it was the house that quickened her pulse. Not the man.

With huge streamlined windows and a curved end like the prow of a ship, the old house was stunning. The glimpse of dark blue ocean glittering beyond it enhanced its beauty, as did the lush garden that hid it from the security gates. Gates that opened as soon as she'd nosed her car off the street.

Had Donato been watching for her, or his security staff? She'd seen no one on the long drive from the street to the clifftop house.

Now there he was under the huge circular portico, his expression unreadable. Against the bright beaten copper of the doors he looked severe. She told herself it was because he wore black trousers and shirt, the sleeves rolled casually up his arms. Yet the contrast between the man and the bright metal behind him reminded her again of that fallen-angel image.

There was nothing casual about his wide stance. Or the way he watched her. Through the windscreen Ella felt the sizzle of his dark eyes. Her skin tingled, her blood a rush of adrenalin as she stared back.

The scary thing about Donato Salazar was the way he saw beyond the surface to the woman she was inside. To the woman she'd never dared let herself be.

Ella had never felt so *naked* as with him. It was as if he saw through a lifetime's defences. He challenged her in a way no man ever had. Donato called to a reckless side she'd never let loose.

For a moment fear pinned her to her seat. Then she thrust open her door and got out, to be instantly enveloped by the summer heat.

Over the car roof their gazes collided and meshed. Ella's pulse racketed and her insides clenched in a way that wasn't about fear but anticipation.

How could she want a man who'd calmly decreed she had to marry him or watch her father ruined?

Setting her shoulders, Ella slammed the door and stalked across the terrace.

He didn't move towards her, just stood: tall, brooding and enigmatic. His hands were shoved deep into his pockets, making him look nonchalant. That only spiked her annoyance.

Even worse, he looked every bit as stunning as he had last night. The muted lighting at the party hadn't exaggerated the wide set of his shoulders or the lean strength of his body. Her gaze skittered over corded forearms, dusted with dark hair, and heavy thigh muscles. For a shaky moment she wondered how it would feel to be held against that hard masculine frame.

Fear skidded down her spine. She didn't do lust. Not like this. And not with a man like Donato Salazar.

He smiled as she approached and the pale scar on one side of his face disappeared into the groove running up his cheek. Just like that white heat shimmered through her feminine core. She blinked, stumbling a little on an uneven flagstone, and reminded herself she was too furious to feel attraction.

Nevertheless, she wished she'd taken time to hunt out a pair of heels so she didn't have to tilt her chin to look at him.

'Ella, you're looking particularly vibrant today.'

'Vibrant?' She shook her head. 'The word is *angry*.'

'It suits you.' His smile didn't falter. If anything he looked satisfied. But despite the smile there was something guarded about his expression. His eyes held secrets.

Not surprising, given the games he played. She'd give an awful lot to know what they were.

What made him tick? What was he after? For the life of her she couldn't believe a man like Donato Salazar really wanted to marry one of Reg Sanderson's daughters. Especially her, the prosaic, sensible, not-a-glamorous-bone-in-her-body one.

She stiffened. This wasn't about her. It was about saving Fuzz and Rob.

'We need to talk.'

'Of course. Come through.' He stepped back and gestured for her to enter.

She strode past him into a wide circular foyer. Her staccato steps petered out as her gaze caught on the perfect curving lines of the staircase to the upper floor. Delicate wrought iron formed a balustrade featuring wood nymphs and fauns dancing up the steps. Pure art deco whimsy.

Ella took a step closer, entranced despite her fury.

Then from behind came the thud of the heavy front doors closing her in. The hairs on her nape stood up and a frisson of anxiety resonated through her.

Ridiculous. She was here because she needed to have this out with him, face to face.

'This way.' Donato was beside her, leading the way towards a sitting room that featured views across a terrace and in-ground pool to the Pacific Ocean beyond.

Ella didn't budge. 'This won't take long.' She planted her feet.

He swung around, eyebrows silently rising. 'You look very combative.'

'You're not surprised.'

He shrugged and walked back to where she stood in the centre of the circular foyer. 'I know you're a volatile woman.'

Ella snorted. Volatile? She was the stable one of the family. The one who never had tantrums. The one who quietly got on with whatever needed to be done. Before she left home it had been she, not her father or older sister, who made sure the housekeeper and gardener received their instructions and their pay.

'I'm not volatile. I'm justifiably annoyed. There's a difference.' She breathed deep, feeling indignation well. 'Or will you decide my reaction is due to the fact I'm female?' That had always been one of her father's favourite put-downs.

Donato raised his hands as if in surrender. Yet

the spark in those dark blue eyes told her he was enjoying himself too much to give in.

'I'm a lot of things, Ella. But not sexist.'

He was far closer than she liked. Too close. Her stomach gave a betraying wobble.

She swallowed hard as the aroma of rich coffee and warm male skin enveloped her. It was as if her body was absorbed in a different conversation than the one coming out of her mouth. A conversation that was about heat and desire and that phantom ache down deep in her womb.

She didn't know how to combat it. Creating distance between them was the obvious option but she wouldn't let him see even a hint of fear. She'd learned young that revealing weakness only made things worse.

'I want to know what's going on.'

'Well, since you opted to come here rather than to Bennelong Point, I've arranged for us to share lunch on the terrace.'

Had she ever met anyone so coolly sure of himself? So infuriating? He cast even her father into the shade with his supreme self-confidence.

Yet, despite her annoyance, Ella didn't get the same feeling from Donato as she did from her father, who so blatantly exulted in triumphing over others. Donato was manipulating her yet she didn't feel bullied. More…*challenged.*

Which showed how dangerous was this undercurrent of attraction humming in her veins. It tempted her to put a pretty gloss on Donato's outrageous demands.

Ella crossed her arms, glaring. 'I didn't come here for lunch.'

'You need to look after yourself. You didn't stop for breakfast, did you?' Donato took a step closer and suddenly the spacious two-storey room shrank around them. Ella breathed deeper, needing oxygen. 'You were still in bed when I rang.' The glint in his dark eyes reminded her of his teasing as she lay naked in bed, and heat drilled down through her belly.

Ella stiffened, ignoring the telltale flush rising in her throat and cheeks.

'I want the truth. You don't *need* to marry Reg Sanderson's daughter. The idea of marriage to cement closer business ties doesn't wash. You're the one my father needs, not the other way around. Why are you playing along with the idea?'

For a millisecond Donato's eyes widened, giving her a glimpse of surprise in a flash of indigo that rivalled the ocean's brilliance. Then his eyelids lowered and his gaze became unreadable.

Ella's breathing quickened. There was something there. Something she'd said, something he didn't expect her to know. But what? She racked her brain but she'd only stated the obvious. She could find no significance there.

Yet she couldn't shake the feeling she'd inadvertently hit on something important.

'Things aren't always as clear-cut as they seem.' Donato paused. 'Your father's proposal has definite advantages.'

Ella jammed her hands on her hips. 'What advantages? Name one.'

In answer Donato's eyes skated down, past the warm blush in her throat, over her loose-fitting top, lightweight trousers and flat sandals.

She'd dressed for comfort rather than sophistication. Her floaty aqua and silver top was a favourite. Now, under Donato's trawling stare, Ella had a qualm that it had somehow suddenly become transparent. Surely his gaze grazed her skin, following every curve the material should have hidden. As if he already knew her intimately.

Already. The word was a promise she couldn't dislodge from her brain.

Ella's body came alive, just as it had last night. She'd told herself that had been an illusion created by tiredness and stress. But she didn't feel tired now. She felt wired, waves of energy ripping through her, awakening every nerve ending.

She jutted her jaw. 'You don't have to marry me to get sex.'

'Why, Ella—' his eyes gleamed with a banked heat and his mouth curved in a slow smile that turned her insides to mush '—that's quite an offer. I'm charmed and delighted.'

For one insane moment she almost smiled back, till her brain processed his words.

'I'm offering nothing.' Her head snapped back, her pulse thrumming at the look in his eyes. 'I'm just stating the obvious. Even if you wanted to go to bed with me, marriage isn't necessary.' Unfortunately her explanation came out in an unsteady rush as he leaned closer.

'Such a tempting idea,' he murmured. 'I'm glad you suggested it.'

'Stop it, Donato. You know I'm not suggesting anything.' But now she couldn't banish the idea of them, together.

'You're thinking about it, aren't you?' His voice

dropped an octave to a warm rumble she felt deep inside. 'I am too, Ella. I find the idea intoxicating.'

He lifted his hand to cup her cheek and sensation juddered through her. Ella shot back a step, her breath snagging. Instead of releasing her, Donato followed, his broad callused palm hot on her skin.

She felt crowded, surrounded.

Excited.

Silence thickened. The saw of her breathing seemed loud, as did the quickened patter of her pulse. But it was the sensations detonating through her body that panicked Ella.

Donato had sabotaged all her erogenous zones, attuning them to his touch. Her lips tingled as his gaze dropped to her mouth. Her nipples budded against the sensible bra she wore, as if mocking her determination *not* to dress up for Donato. Her silky top stirred as she hauled in deeper breaths, the touch of fabric a barely there caress. And between her legs…

Ella swallowed hard, drowning in the slumberous heat of those searing eyes.

'Let me go, Donato.' Her voice was as shaky as she felt. Not with fear, but because her body came alive so instantly, so completely, at his touch.

With every atom of her being she was aware of

his big frame mere inches from her own. It was as if he projected a force-field that sent shock waves across her skin and deeper, heating her core.

'No.' He shook his head. 'I've waited too long.' His palm slid down her cheek to caress her jaw then thrust back into her hair. Ella's neck arched and she bit down a sigh at the luxurious feel of his fingers against her scalp. Tiny little shivers coursed down her back and shoulders.

'Rubbish.' Her voice was far too soft. She cleared her throat and tried to summon the energy to move away. Her knees had grown wobbly. 'We haven't known each other a day.'

Remarkable to think it was less than twenty-four hours since they met.

Donato bent his head even closer and Ella's breath hitched. He held her captive with that remarkable dark blue gaze. 'It's still been too long. I've wanted you since the moment I saw you.' The words were pure seduction, low and tantalising.

Ella told herself it was just a line he tossed out, but even then she couldn't dredge up the power to move. Stunned, she teetered on the brink of losing herself. She swallowed, her mouth drying at what she read in his stare.

'Don't take me for a fool, Donato.' Despite her

indignation her tongue slowed on his name, savouring it. She looked up into that austere, scarred, compelling face and wished, for once in her life, that she really *was* the beauty in the family. The sort to turn even this man's head. 'You came to the party expecting my sister, not me.'

'And how pleased I was that she couldn't make it.' The words were a caress.

'No!' She jerked back, finally breaking from his hold. 'Don't pretend you were bowled over by my looks or my glittering personality. It won't work.' Ella had learned long ago, growing up in her sister's shadow, that she wasn't the sort to turn male heads. Pain twisted, razor-sharp, in her chest.

'You don't believe me, sweet Ella?'

Damn the man. Even that easy endearment sent her heart tumbling. Was she really that needy? So ready to be seduced by a show of attention?

Yet even as she lashed up indignation she knew she was fooling herself. Despite her protests that sense of connection between them was as real as it was inexplicable. It had slammed through her the moment she'd turned to find Donato's eyes on her at the party. It had sung in her veins as she'd sparred with him under her father's horrified gaze. It had turned her on as she lay naked in bed, wishing he was there with her instead of taunting her with that sultry deep voice over the phone.

'Don't toy with me, Donato.' She pressed her lips together.

'You don't trust me, do you?'

Her chin hiked up. 'Not an inch.'

'Maybe this will convince you.' He grabbed her hand and, before she could yank it free, placed it on his chest.

Instantly she stilled. The hard staccato beat of his heart pounded beneath her palm. It wasn't the steady pulse of a man in control. It was the rapid pulse of a man on the brink. Her eyes widened.

Runnels of fire traced across Ella's skin as she met eyes the colour of twilight. His gaze bored into her, challenging yet, incredibly it seemed, honest.

'I want you, Ella.' His gaze pinioned her. 'And you want me.'

Before she could form a reply his big hand lifted to the upper slope of her breast, palm down. 'See? We match.'

It was true. Her heartbeat careered just as fast as his. And all she could think about was how it would feel if he slid his hand just a little lower, to cup her breast.

A hot chill raced through her and desire spiked. Her breath grew ragged.

As if reading her mind, Donato slipped his hand down to cover her breast. Ella bit her lip to shut in a gasp of delight. But she couldn't stop herself from pressing nearer, eyes closing as his hand moulded her soft flesh. Something like relief welled.

He moved and her eyes snapped open. Gripping her arm, he stepped in against her, powering her back until her spine collided with something solid.

They stood toe to toe, hip to thigh, torso to torso and she shivered at how good that felt. Even the scent of him in her nostrils was delicious. The sheer potency of his big body was a promise and, she realised belatedly, a threat.

'No!' She lifted her hands to his shoulders and pushed. He didn't budge. He was as immovable as the Harbour Bridge. 'I don't care what deal you and my father have sewn up. You can't *force* me. Let me go!'

His jaw set and she watched that pulse throb at his temple. He breathed deep, his nostrils flaring. Then, to her surprise, he stepped back. He stood just inches away, his breath hot on her face, the force-field of his body making her flesh prickle and spark.

'This isn't about any deal, Ella. This is about us.'

'There is no *us*.'

'Of course there is. You feel it too, the awareness between us. The desire.'

She felt it all right. It scared her as nothing else ever had that she could recall.

'You think having sex will convince me to marry you?' Her chest rose and fell with her choppy breathing. 'You think you're that good in bed? Or are you relying on blackmail to force me since my sister is out of reach?'

'Don't be a coward, Ella.'

She stiffened. One thing she'd stopped being long ago was a coward. After the life she'd had to endure with her father, the continual battle for respect since love was denied her, she'd earned the right to hold her head high.

'I'm no coward.' It came out through clenched teeth.

'You're looking for excuses.' Donato raised his hands. 'Forget your father. Forget the wedding and the business deal. Forget your sister. I was never interested in her.'

Ella scrutinised his face but his look was sincere. His gaze zeroed in on her mouth and she swallowed hard.

'This is about you and me. I'm telling you I want you. The question is, are you woman enough to admit you want me too?'

'With you holding my father's potential bankruptcy over our heads?'

Donato shook his head. 'There are two separate issues here.' He spoke slowly, his eyes never leaving hers. 'There's my business deal with your father, and yes, the proposal for a wedding is tied to that. But,' he continued when she would have interrupted, 'that's not what we're discussing right now. No one is forcing you into anything. Believe me, I would *never* force a woman into my bed.'

Ella stared into his face, noting how those dark features set in stern lines of rigid control. There was hauteur in the flash of his eyes and pride in the set of his shoulders.

She believed him. The realisation rocked her.

'What we're discussing now is sex.' His voice turned deep and liquid on the word, matching the slow-burning need inside Ella. 'You and me. Uncomplicated, satisfying, scorching.'

'Scorching?' Ella didn't know how the word escaped. It wasn't what she'd meant to say. Clearly the look in his eyes had incinerated part of her brain. 'You assume a lot.'

He shook his head. 'I assume nothing. I *know*, Ella. Can't you feel it?' Again he reached for her, but this time he only clasped her hand lightly. Fire sparked from the point of contact and she had to work to suppress shivers of delight.

How had she come to this? She'd raced halfway across Sydney to confront Donato, filled with righteous indignation and—

But there'd been more, hadn't there? No matter what she pretended, it hadn't just been indignation. She'd been almost *relieved* for the excuse to see him again, despite her fine talk about them never meeting again. She was angry, for sure. But she was also…enthralled.

She swallowed, her throat scratchy as she confronted the truth. She wanted Donato Salazar as she'd never wanted any man. Her skin felt too tight, her chest too full.

Donato stroked one finger along her palm and she gasped as pleasure rocketed through her.

'Tell me you feel it too,' he purred.

Ella bit back a groan of despair. She was out of her depth. She'd never been good at flirtation. Suddenly she didn't care about pride or keeping up an image. This was about survival—and she felt like she was going under for the third time.

'What do you want from me, Donato? I don't play these games.'

'I don't play games either. Not about this.' His face was grim, the hint of teasing erased from features that looked pared back and intense. He swallowed, his Adam's apple bobbing hard, and something within her eased at that visible sign that he wasn't totally in control.

Suddenly he stepped back, releasing her hand, and cool air wafted between them.

'What happens next is up to you.' His heavy-lidded look was a challenge and an invitation.

CHAPTER SEVEN

DONATO LOOKED DOWN into stunning blue-grey eyes, grown huge and wary. He felt the doubt radiating from Ella, just as he felt the heat of her sexual arousal.

His body was taut, humming with need. He couldn't quite believe the effort it took not to step closer and persuade her into surrender as he knew he could. The attraction dragging at his belly, arcing between them, was powerful.

But there'd been something about the way she'd mentioned her sister, on top of her talk of being forced, that held him back. He'd seen the quickly veiled hint of fragility in Ella's expression.

He didn't have her measure yet but one thing he knew. He needed Ella to come to him.

The moment of silence grew to two pulse beats, three, four, more. His nerves and his patience stretched. He forced himself to stand there unmoving, as if he wasn't strung out.

Then, with what sounded like a muffled oath,

Ella launched herself forward. She cannoned into him, soft and curvaceous, warm and delectably feminine. Automatically he grabbed her to him, catching her in a tight hold. Her arms looped over his shoulders, her hands burrowing up through his hair, pulling his head down.

He had a moment to register that fresh-as-a-garden-after-rain scent then their mouths collided and his brain shorted.

So good. She felt even better than he'd expected. And she tasted—

Donato plunged deep into her mouth, forcing her head back, swallowing her sigh of response. Ribbons of heat unfurled through him as he savoured Ella, so delicious, so right. Her soft lips, her demanding tongue, the way she melted into him even as she challenged him to give more. He angled his head, hauling her even closer, lost in a kiss that was so much more than he'd expected, despite his anticipation.

He couldn't get enough. Her lush body cushioning his instant erection. Her hot, eager mouth that tasted of peach nectar. Her thigh, sliding restlessly against his leg as their tongues tangled and lips fused.

Donato grabbed her thigh and hauled it up, swallowing her gasp of shocked approval. There. He wanted her there. He bent his knees, angling his hips so he rubbed against the softest, most secret part of her.

To his delight Ella's hands tightened against his scalp, not pushing him away but clutching as if she couldn't get close enough.

Dimly he wondered what had happened to slow seduction. To years of expertise at pleasing a woman. To caution and taking things one step at a time.

With Ella there were no steps. There was just a headlong plunge into riotous need.

With his other hand he grabbed her backside, lifting her into him, and she purred her approval. That throaty sound incited, inviting more. She nipped his bottom lip and angled her head to taste him better and his head spun.

Yes! He'd known Ella wouldn't be a shrinking violet. Not the way passion had sparked and simmered in her, a conflagration waiting to be ignited. Yet he hadn't expected—

Thought died as she rolled her pelvis against him.

Hell! He was shaking all over. If he wasn't careful he might drop her.

No, he couldn't drop her. His hands were welded to her. But they might collapse together on the marble floor if his legs gave way. He was pretty sure he could still enjoy Ella, even with a concussion. In fact a concussion would be worth it to experience Ella coming apart around him.

But she might get hurt.

With a desperate effort he dragged his eyelids up. He couldn't remember shutting his eyes. All he remembered was the sensual assault as she launched herself at him and his body going into meltdown.

Lips still locked with hers, Donato scanned the foyer, instantly discounting the stairs to the upper floor and the bedrooms. They'd never make it that far. At this rate he wasn't sure they'd make it out of their clothes.

The sideboard. It sat between two doors, a collector's piece of exquisite workmanship. Perfect.

Lifting Ella against him, he stumbled across the foyer. Her eyes snapped open, the blaze hitting like a punch to the solar plexus.

'What?' She tugged her head away and instantly Donato wanted her back, her mouth surrendering to his.

Then she must have felt the solid furniture behind her because understanding flickered in her eyes. Donato lifted her so she sat on the sideboard, then he stepped in, pushing her knees wide.

For the merest of moments there was stillness between them, a waiting awareness, a final chance to break apart. Then Ella's eyes drifted shut as he lightly touched her breast. It was high and plump enough to fill his hand. Delectable. Just like her shuddering sigh of approval and the way she arched into his touch, eager for more.

Donato smiled grimly. She was so responsive. He wanted to tease and pleasure her, but he wasn't sure he could manage anything like his usual finesse.

Then Ella's hand closed over him and his vision blurred, his groin tightening. All the blood in his body rushed south. Need rocked him and dimly he wondered if he'd have time to get free of his trousers before he came.

Instinct took over from thought as their mouths met and fused. She tugged his head down again, as if afraid he might pull back. Donato ravaged her mouth, forgetting all about control in the need to crush her close.

Between them hands scrabbled at clothes, fumbling and tangling.

Ella's fingers against his erection almost destroyed Donato. He grabbed her hand and planted it against his chest, over his thundering heart. Then he was wrenching at her trousers, hauling down the zip as she wriggled, helping him. His hands were unsteady but soon there was warm silken skin beneath his touch. Seconds later he was free of his own constraining trousers and pulling her to him.

Carajo! Had anything, ever, felt so good?

Donato lifted his head to drag in oxygen, his lungs already overloaded. Her eyes opened and he was lost in the silvery dazzle of her stare.

Then he touched her with one finger, circling, probing, and her eyes slitted to diamond-bright shards, her throat arching back as if her head was too heavy. Ella was soft, warm, wet, shifting restlessly as one finger became two and—

'Condom.' The word was a wisp of sound he almost missed. Then Ella straightened, her eyes locking with his. 'I don't have one.' Delicate colour climbed her throat, a contrast to the pure silver of her eyes. 'I didn't think…'

Donato was fascinated by the suspicion that Ella was embarrassed, this woman who'd launched herself at him without reservation, so for a moment the implication didn't hit. When it did he jerked back, stunned.

How had he, of all people, forgotten anything so basic? Such thoughtlessness wasn't part of his DNA. Not now, not ever.

It was the work of seconds to grab the foil packet from his trouser pocket and rip it open. See? What seemed a lifetime ago he'd had foresight. He just hadn't been prepared for the cataclysm that was Ella Sanderson in his arms.

There was something unbelievably arousing about holding Ella's gaze as he sheathed himself. The soft pink rose to streak her fine cheekbones. For a fraction of a second the word *endearing* flashed into Donato's brain, before higher thought became impossible and he gave in to primitive instinct.

Hands to her smooth bare hips, he pulled her close then with one sure movement pushed home.

A sound halfway between a sigh and a sob escaped Ella's reddened lips and he made himself still, though the tight embrace of her slick heat almost made him lose himself.

Had he hurt her? He tried to unlock his jaw to ask but if he moved a muscle he mightn't be able to hold back from the inevitable.

Then Ella shifted, her legs lifting over his hips, locking around his waist, making him sink deeper into beckoning warmth. She clung to his shoulders and suddenly there was nothing stopping him. That was invitation in her eyes, not pain. And the feel of her moving against him…

Donato succumbed, taking her fast and hard, revelling in her beautiful body that accepted him so eagerly. Each tilt of her pelvis, each softly in-drawn breath was an incitement to pleasure. He couldn't get enough. He couldn't manage finesse. There was nothing but the compulsion to make her his in the most primitive, satisfying way possible.

The world was already blurring when Donato felt the ripples of her arousal quicken around him. The sensation was too much and he braced one arm on the wall behind her, bucking high and hard with a desperation that was more animal than civilised man.

He needed her, and this exquisite pleasure.

'Ella!' Her name was a husky roar, surprising him as it emerged from his mouth.

Her body stiffened then jerked around him. Her eyes sprang wide open and he fell into pools of burnished moonlight.

There was a flash of heat, a surge of energy

and he spilled himself, collapsing into her as the world exploded. Chest and shoulders heaving, head bowed against her fragrant neck, Donato experienced pure rapture as Ella clutched him close.

He'd expected passion and pleasure. But nothing like this. When had he ever called out a lover's name like that? When had he ever forgotten protection?

Donato gathered her in, relishing her soft womanly body, so lax in his arms.

The world had contracted to the living pulse beating through her, through him, filling the air around them and the darkness behind her closed lids. Ella wasn't sure she was still alive after that cataclysmic orgasm.

Had it ever been like that before?

Of course it hadn't. If it had she'd never have let her love life sink without a trace.

Donato moved, pulling gently away, murmuring something she couldn't hear over her rocketing pulse and harsh breathing. Soon she'd open her eyes but for now she slumped back against the wall that at this moment felt as comfortable as any feather bed.

Her bones had melted. She wasn't sure she could

move her legs. But it didn't matter. She never wanted to move again. She felt blissfully, utterly wonderful.

She felt… Words faded in the afterglow of rapture.

Finally, the awkward angle of her head against the wall and the hard surface beneath her penetrated her dazed brain. She should move. She had…surely there was something she had to do?

Gingerly Ella sat up, hands braced on the seat beneath her, only to find it wasn't a seat. It was hard and bumpy. With a huge effort she pried open heavy eyelids and looked down. She was sitting on a carving of a chariot. It was pulled by horses with wide nostrils and, as she shifted, she saw a couple of naked men, maybe gods, riding behind.

Ella blinked, her hands stroking the satiny polished wood beyond the carved plaque. Her gaze strayed to the delicate, obviously hand-carved garlands of fruit and flowers that grew fancifully out of the top of the sideboard to trail decoratively down the front.

Her throat closed. If she wasn't mistaken she'd just had mind-blowing sex on top of a piece of furniture worth more than she earned in a year.

A museum piece that some collector had no doubt lovingly restored.

Her fingers tightened on the edge of the brilliantly polished wood. Her eyes closed.

Forget the furniture, Ella. How about the fact you had wild sex with a stranger? A man you've known less than a day? And you barely made it past his front door?

She swallowed hard, her throat constricting as her body hummed with the resonance of the climax they'd shared.

Who was this woman and what had she done with Ella Sanderson?

A footstep sounded and her eyes popped open. Relief made her sag, her hand to her racing heart. 'It's you.'

'You were expecting someone else?' Donato looked as debonair and dangerous as ever. More so, with his thick black hair deliciously rumpled. A shiver spread out from her womb and she kept her eyes off his face, not ready to meet that intense scrutiny.

He was fully clothed. Ella tugged her long top lower. But that voice in her head drawled that it was too late for modesty. That didn't stop the blood rushing to her face as she registered her bare legs and the fact she still wore her shoes. Her pants lay in a heap a few steps away.

She swallowed, reminding herself that embarrassment couldn't kill her. It never had in all those years facing her father's superior friends. Even this, the pinnacle of mortification, would pass.

'I wondered if you have staff.'

'Not today. I gave them the day off.' He paced closer and her head jerked up. The gleam in his eyes was pure carnal invitation, as was the half smile flirting at the corners of his mouth. Heat blasted her, turning the marrow in her bones molten.

How could she feel so needy again? Surely it had only been minutes since they'd— Ella slammed a door on that train of thought.

He was before her now, his palms resting lightly on her bare thighs. His hands were broad, hard with calluses, and the feel of them on her skin made her pulse skitter. She remembered him touching her intimately and the breath sighed out of her lungs.

Then his words penetrated.

'You gave them the day off? Why? Because you were so sure we'd…' Ella swallowed hard. 'So sure of *me*?'

His expression was still, giving nothing away, except for that banked heat.

'I was sure that, whatever happened, I wanted complete privacy. No distractions.'

She angled her jaw. 'In case I ravished you before I even got past the foyer?' Her bravado hid a world of discomfort. She wanted to scurry away and hide, not brazen out her inexplicable behaviour. She'd acted like a tart instead of her cautious, reserved self.

'I've discovered I adore being ravished in the foyer.' His fingers touched her chin, tilting it towards him. 'And it was a mutual ravishment, Ella.'

Did he say that to make her feel better? It didn't.

She'd known from the first that he was Trouble with a capital T. She just hadn't reckoned on her own body betraying her. In twenty-six years it had never done so before. Sex, in her admittedly limited experience, had been carefully planned, horizontal and…nice. Not a blaze of out-of-control libidos.

Something flared in Donato's eyes and she just knew he was thinking about it too. Sex. The scent of it hung in the air and, despite her lassitude mere minutes ago, Ella's body was ripe and ready for him again.

She shifted back on the sideboard, yanking her chin from his touch.

'I need to get dressed.'

For an answer his hand slid slowly up her thigh, creating waves of tingling pleasure. 'No need for that. Let's go somewhere more comfortable.' His eyes had that heavy-lidded look that made her pulse race. His voice had dropped to a low burr of temptation.

Insidious longing filled Ella and she slapped her hand on his to stop him reaching up under her top. She didn't trust herself to resist if he touched her *there*.

'No!' She breathed deep. 'I want to get dressed.'

His fingers splayed wide on her thighs, curling around them, sending awareness rippling through her. The tension in her belly notched higher.

'This isn't over, Ella.' His head lowered towards hers, his breath hazing her lips. 'Don't pretend it is.'

Was that a threat or a promise? It stiffened her spine, giving her the strength to shove him back with the flat of her hand. For a moment she thought he wouldn't move, then his fingers trailed down her thighs and away as he took a pace back.

Ella shimmied to the edge of the sideboard and

onto the floor. Her knees wobbled for a perilous moment but she forced herself to stand tall. Just as if she paraded half naked before men on a regular basis.

'Don't hide from the truth, Ella. Amazing as it was, that barely touched the surface, for either of us.' His swift, all-encompassing survey left her blood singing.

Looking him in the face was far harder than facing her stressed manager in a foul mood, or her father in full flight. 'I'd prefer to have this conversation with my clothes on. You have the advantage over me there.'

The slow curve of his lips did devastating things to her and the devilish glint in his eyes was even worse. She sank back against the sideboard, needing support.

'You want me naked?' His hand went to the top button of his shirt and Ella swallowed hard. Of course she wanted him naked. He was right. She hadn't had nearly enough of him.

'I want my clothes.' Her voice was too strident but it was the best she could do. Dragging her gaze from his to the discarded heap of fabric on the floor, she moved forward.

'If you must.' Before she could get there Donato

had scooped up not only her trousers, but her cotton undies too. They dangled from his fingers—plain and ordinary, just like her. She'd challenged herself this morning *not* to dig out her sexy lace knickers and bra, bought on a whim and worn once. To do so would have been an admission that she fancied him. That she wanted him to think of her as alluring. Well, the laugh was on her. Instead of black lace, he had his hands on beige cotton.

Ella met his eyes and refused to blush. She held out her hand.

'They're still warm from your body.' Just like that he cut her off at the knees, swiping away the last tatters of her hard-won dignity. He sounded pleased. He didn't sound like a man taking no for an answer.

She grabbed them from him and, following the direction he gestured, strode across the marble floor to the sanctuary of a bathroom.

Donato watched her stride across to the cloakroom, enjoying every step. He shifted, erect just at the sight of those beautiful long legs and the tantalising glimpses of her pale bare backside as her long top swayed from side to side. Her head was up and her shoulders back as if she owned the world. Such a contrast to the blushing woman who'd found it hard to meet his eyes a minute before.

Ella Sanderson was a conundrum. She was the hottest woman he'd ever had. Just talking to her turned him on. And she was so passionate. Yet there was a reserve about her, and there'd been no mistaking the shock in her eyes at what they'd done.

He ploughed his hand back through his hair. He was shocked too. Not because they'd had sex. That had been inevitable. But that it had been so earth-shattering. And that it left him needy, desperate to have her again.

There was something else about Ella too. A hint of vulnerability despite her sassy mouth. In fact that mouth of hers deserved close study over a long period. It gave her away, he realised. Any man could see it was the mouth of a temptress. But it trembled just a little when she was unsure of herself. And she *had* been unsure.

More than once that suggestion of a tremor had made him stop and rethink. He'd bet Ella would hate that, if she knew.

She challenged him more effectively than anyone he knew. He loved sparring with her, waiting to see what she came out with. She was a delight.

That moment when she'd stood there, half naked, gnawing her lip and patently regretting what they'd done, Ella had still had the sass to imply she'd been the sexual aggressor.

As if he hadn't been the one forcing her to confront her own desire!

Donato's lips quirked. Had she worn that ugly underwear to keep him at bay? He found himself curious to see what her bra was like. She had a voluptuous body, no matter how she tried to hide it with that shapeless top. Her rounded hips were made to entice a man. She was slim and lithe but she had the sort of curves that made a man glad he was male. He looked forward to having her naked in his bed.

There was a click and the door opened. She stepped out, fully dressed and in control. The wanton woman hidden beneath her shapeless top; even her hair was yanked back in a ponytail. But the skylight above allowed diffused sunlight to catch the tones of honey and caramel in her soft brown hair. Her chin was up, ready for confrontation, and Donato stepped forward, his pulse quickening.

This time she met his gaze head-on. Instantly he felt that crackle, as electricity splintered the air.

It took him a moment to realise her eyes were

once more that intriguing shade of blue-grey. For a few moments, when she'd shattered around him, her eyes had been pure molten silver.

Donato began calculating how long it would be before he saw that precious shimmer again.

CHAPTER EIGHT

THEY SAT AT a glass-topped table on the shady pool terrace. Ella didn't know whether it was the luxury of her deeply upholstered chair, the glass of chilled Semillon Donato had poured or his air of ease but, remarkably, she began to relax.

Almost as if that hectic interlude in the foyer had never happened.

No, not that. She was hyper-aware of him—every move, every look. The shimmering excitement in her belly had eased a little, but not vanished.

Yet something had shifted. The challenge was no longer overt but overlaid with what felt curiously like understanding. Or a truce.

There'd been no provocative comments since she emerged from the bathroom. No double entendres. No confrontation and definitely no smirking from Donato.

He'd ushered her out here, chatting easily as if they hadn't just imploded in each other's arms. Maybe that should have insulted her, but Ella was relieved, feeling some of her jittery tension drain away.

She'd settled at the table, relieved to be off her unsteady legs, and watched him uncover a feast. The sort that took hours, and professional chefs, to prepare.

She should be critically analysing every nuance of the situation, working out how to counter the threat Donato posed.

It was a measure of the strangeness of the day, and of his easy charm, that Ella simply gave in to hunger and ate.

The food was delicious. There were tiny melt-in-the-mouth lobster patties, crispbread bites with prawns and aioli, a colourful salad decorated with fresh mango, and an array of other delicacies.

Had Donato snapped his fingers and ordered a banquet? Did he offer such feasts to all the women he seduced?

Her breath shortened. He hadn't needed to seduce anyone today, had he? She'd been primed and ready for him.

He refilled their glasses and Ella's gaze fixed on his well-shaped hands and sinewy forearms, strong and dusted with dark hair. He was so blatantly enticing. Something dropped hard in her belly.

Fantastic sex as an antidote to life's problems? If only it were that simple.

'Are we going to talk about it?' She pushed her plate away. 'Or are we going to ignore the elephant in the room?'

A long dimple carved Donato's cheek and a chord in her chest tweaked hard. So much for burning off the passion he'd aroused. Instead her susceptibility had increased.

Ella blinked, stunned but somehow not surprised. She'd never been into casual sex. And for her there'd been nothing casual about today, though she wouldn't examine just what that meant.

'You think of sex as an elephant?' he murmured.

Her lips twitched despite her resolve.

'Don't be obtuse.' She reached for her glass and took a sip. The crisp wine was delicious against her suddenly dry throat. 'We've resolved nothing. I—'

'Of course we have.' His smile grew and he gave her *that* look. The one that made her feel as if she didn't know her own body any more. 'We've confirmed that you and I are every bit as good together as we'd assumed.'

His eyes didn't leave her face but heat licked her in all sorts of hidden places. He lifted his glass in silent salute and drank. Ella was left wondering how the sight of that tanned throat working as he swallowed could create a squall of such hectic need in her.

She shook her head.

'Don't play coy, Ella. You wondered right from the start how we'd be together.'

Ella firmed her lips. 'Don't try to distract me, Donato. It won't work.'

The glint in his dark eyes and the quizzically raised eyebrow told her he disagreed. She put her glass down with a click and sat straighter.

'You said this morning you still want this marriage.' She couldn't bring herself to say *marry me*. It was just too far-fetched. 'Why? There's nothing you'd gain by it.'

His raised eyebrow shot even higher.

Ella put up her hand. 'We've already demonstrated you don't need marriage for sex.'

Would he make a quip about that? She'd laid herself open to it. But no, he merely sipped his wine.

'How about an introduction to Sydney society?' He tilted his head to one side as if sharing a confidence. She didn't believe it.

'You hardly need that.'

'Don't I?' He leaned back further, lounging casually as if they discussed nothing more important than the ship passing far out to sea, or the rainbow lorikeets clustering in the ancient Port Jackson fig tree at the bottom of the garden.

Ella wanted to grab him by the collar and shake him till he lost that complacent look. Or kiss him. She shoved the thought aside. She was already in enough strife.

'Of course not. You've got the money and influence to open any door.' Just look at this house. Whether he owned or rented it, it cost a bomb.

'But you know I also have a criminal record. I served time in juvenile detention, then prison.' Did she imagine his mouth thinned on the words? Though his expression remained unreadable, his face looked somehow more severe.

'So?'

'It hasn't occurred to you that someone with my background might find doors still closed to him? That some people are uncomfortable mixing with an ex-con? A *dangerous* ex-con.'

Dangerous. There was that word again.

Yet would a truly dangerous man have treated her as he had?

She'd disintegrated at his touch, thrown herself at him, behaved with a reckless carnality that even now took her breath away. Yet not once had he tried to force her, though it was obvious he wielded power as easily as she did a thermometer. Though he'd challenged her from the moment they'd met, she'd never relinquished the right to choose. If anything, he'd emphasised that, leaving it to her to bridge the gap between them.

Nor had he made her feel cheap. He'd reminded her it had been a *mutual* seduction.

Ella thought of Donato's hand at her back as she'd walked out here on legs that threatened to give way, how he'd given her time to come back to herself after their tumultuous lovemaking.

Donato Salazar, ruthless tycoon, the man who held her father in the palm of his hand, had been *kind.*

And not because he wanted something. She'd already given him what he wanted back in the foyer, with her legs around his waist and her hands clutching him close.

He was far more than the dangerous predator she'd first imagined.

Ella remembered something she'd read on the Net last night. About how there'd been virtually no turnover in his personal staff, about the loyalty he inspired. She'd assumed he paid well. Now she wondered if it was more complex, more to do with the man himself.

Ella stared, mesmerised by the hint of tension in Donato's shoulders.

Was it true? Were there really doors still barred to him?

She couldn't believe he let the opinions of others matter. There was something so *sure* about him, so adamantine.

'You're saying you want to marry into my family to gain respectability?' She frowned. Her father had been part of elite Sydney society for years but his position had slipped. There were some who disapproved of him and his flashy ways.

'Is that so unbelievable?'

'Frankly? Yes.'

He said nothing. Impatience rose.

'So you're not going to tell me what's going on?'

Eyes the colour of twilight held hers. Their colour seemed to darken as she watched. It must be a trick of the light. But there was no mistaking the subtle change in his expression. It grew shuttered.

Moments ago she'd flirted with the idea Donato wasn't nearly as scary as imagination had painted him. That illusion vanished now. He looked as unsentimental as the worst corporate raider.

Except there was more. Ella felt again the heat of his possession. That current of electricity. That *connection.* She couldn't believe, after a lifetime dealing with her self-serving, merciless father, that she'd respond this way to a man who was just the same. Her sixth sense told her there was a lot more to Donato.

Briskly she rubbed her hands over her arms, trying to smooth her prickling flesh.

'Why don't you tell me the truth? Why insist on this farce of a marriage?' Her voice rose as disappointment vied with frustration. Had she really hoped things had changed because they'd been intimate?

Heat streaked Ella's cheeks and she turned, staring across the lush garden to the sea beyond. She wasn't used to these games. She wasn't used to casual sex and its aftermath. Donato had provoked her and she'd let anger and desire lead her out of her depth.

She should be home now, washing clothes for work next week. Or scouting the sales and second-hand furniture stores for another lost treasure to restore.

Donato leaned forward and involuntarily her

gaze slewed to his. Something kicked in her chest as the air thickened.

It's too late. The damage is done. You can't turn back the clock. He fascinates you and you still want him.

Ella reached for her wine glass then let her hand drop. It wasn't alcohol she needed. Her head was fuzzy enough without it.

'The truth is rarely simple, *cariño*. And not always desirable.'

Was it the unexpected lilting endearment that caught at Ella's throat? Or the expression on Donato's face? That fleeting hint of emotion stilled Ella's heart. She stared, wondering if she'd imagined it. But there'd been no mistaking the stark pain she'd glimpsed. It stunned her.

'You want the truth?' He shook his head, muttering something that might be Spanish. It had those fluid cadences. Then he sat forward, his elbows on his knees as he filled her personal space. 'The truth is—I want this wedding your father is planning.'

She should have been insulted. Despite their sexual attraction, he didn't want marriage for the sake of marrying *her*. He'd been just as willing to marry Fuzz. Instead Ella was intrigued. There was something there. Something she couldn't put her finger on, that would explain everything if only she understood.

He wanted the wedding.

Not *her*, but the wedding.

Ella frowned, testing the notion that Donato would marry a stranger, a total stranger, just to secure a place in society. It didn't make sense.

'Stop scowling, Ella. You'll give yourself a headache.'

'You don't think the idea of being forced into marriage is enough to make my head hurt?' She couldn't believe he'd do it. It was too preposterous.

To Ella's surprise, Donato reached out and took her hand, clasping it loosely. 'It will be all right.' His voice was low and reassuring, like a wave of soft warmth. 'All you need to know is that while the wedding plans go ahead so does my support for your father.'

For a heady moment she wanted to sink against him, trust that it really would be all right. But how could that be?

'Except you're threatening him.' And, as a result, the rest of her family.

'You care so much about his money? You're dependent on it?'

Her eyebrows arched. She hadn't been dependent on Reg Sanderson's money since the day she turned seventeen and walked out of the door to pursue her own life. It didn't matter that her dreams were mundane by her father's standards. Becoming a nurse, doing something concrete and practical to help people. Being financially independent. Choosing her own friends. All those things had been important milestones.

'I care that you think you can blackmail me into marriage. It's not ethical.' She speared him with a look and tugged to free her hand from his grip. It didn't work and she shot to her feet.

Donato rose at the same time, looming close. 'You want ethics from me? From an ex-crim?' His jaw set.

'Why not?' Ella should be intimidated by the glint in his eyes and by the way he crowded her, his wide shoulders hemming her in. Instead she felt a delicious thrill as she arched her neck to hold his gaze. With Donato she'd never felt more starkly the divide between male and female. She revelled in his size, his brooding presence and the unfamiliar sensation of being almost petite.

Was she insane?

'You're not a thug, Donato.' There was too much

intense thought behind his alert gaze for that to be true. And too much control—it was stamped on his features. Then there was the way he'd made love to her…

For the first time it seemed words eluded him. He stared as if he'd never seen her like before.

What? Had he really thought she'd have given herself to a man she feared?

'You don't say,' he said at last. 'And you're an expert on thugs? Growing up in a north-shore mansion and attending a posh private school?' His words were a silky taunt and she wondered at the anger she'd inadvertently stirred. Because she refused to think the worst of him? Had she questioned too closely?

'You *did* check on me.' Ella blinked, amazed at how betrayed she felt. She tasted disappointment, a bitter tang on her tongue.

Donato frowned. 'I said I hadn't. It doesn't take an investigator to know your father wouldn't send his darling daughter anywhere she'd mix with the wrong sort.'

Ella's stomach swooped in relief. She hadn't wanted to believe Donato had lied.

She huffed a mirthless laugh. She'd never been Reg's 'darling daughter'. If only Donato knew, her school had had its share of bullies. Maybe if she'd been pretty or pert or less studious they wouldn't have targeted her.

'I've met some thugs in my time.' Her father being one. 'They bully those who seem weaker. But really they're cowards, scared of anyone stronger.'

'Yet you don't think of me as a bully?'

Ella drew a deep breath, then wished she hadn't as she dragged in his spicy warm scent. It made her want to kiss that hard beautiful mouth. She dragged her hand free and stepped back, her chair grating across the flagstones.

'No, I don't.' Donato was demanding, arrogant, clever and ruthless. But he'd been considerate, reassuring and almost…tender. He'd kept his word, refusing to have her investigated because he knew the idea revolted her. He'd been honest, up to a point.

'Tell me about the man you attacked.'

Donato's head reared back. 'What makes you think I want to talk about that?'

She shrugged. 'Why wouldn't you? Don't tell me you're scared I'll judge you?'

Instead of bridling at the taunt, Donato surveyed her with a thoroughness that brought all that reckless awareness straight to the surface in a blaze like wildfire.

Ignoring the flare of arousal, she stared straight back. She needed to understand him.

'Why did you fight with him?'

He shrugged, his expression closed. 'He deserved it. He hurt someone.'

Ella frowned. She hadn't read about anyone else in the fight, just the teenage Donato and a forty-year-old man. Yet it had been the older man carted off to hospital after the police intervened.

'So you were protecting someone?' Her chest contracted at the idea of a teenager taking on a grown man to save someone else.

She'd never had a protector in her life, had always fought her own battles, but the idea held huge appeal. Perhaps *because* no one had ever stood up for her. It made his actions more understandable, more forgivable.

Ella counted one breath, two, three, before finally he shook his head.

'It wasn't that simple. Don't imagine I'm some hero.' His mouth twisted harshly. 'I'm not.'

Her thoughts stalled at his tone, and at that flash of dark emotion. He looked…tortured. And she'd swear she heard desolation in his stark words.

Then, even as the impression formed, his expression was wiped clear.

But that split second had been enough to set Ella's thoughts whirling.

Did he blame himself for not protecting this other person? Clearly *something* still ate at him, despite the passage of time. Donato was in his mid-thirties, yet long-ago hurt was buried beneath all that surface sangfroid.

Whatever he felt in that carefully guarded soul, it ran deep and strong.

Instead of frightening her, the knowledge drew her. She wanted to smooth her hands over his set shoulders, press herself against him and learn all there was to know about Donato Salazar.

Fear jolted through her. Fear of how much she wanted to break down that wall of superior calm and find the man behind it.

You haven't known him a day and already you want so much!

Alarm made her voice abrupt. 'Is that the only time you've been violent?'

'What is this, an interview?'

Ella notched her chin high. '*You're* the one talking about marriage.'

'I've never been violent towards a woman. It's not something you have to worry about.'

'Because you say so?' She crossed her arms over her chest.

'It's not something I'd ever do.' Indignation flashed in his eyes, but it was the proud set of his chin, the distaste in his flared nostrils and flat mouth that told her she'd struck a nerve. 'I was brought up to respect women. You have nothing to fear from me.'

Scary how easy it was for her to believe him.

'What about men?'

'If you were a man we wouldn't be having this conversation.' His voice dropped to the deep, resonant pitch that made her want to do something crazy, like drag his head down to hers and kiss him till he told her all his secrets.

She made herself take a single step back from him. His jaw tightened.

'You haven't answered my question.'

'Am I physically dangerous?' He sighed and shook his head. 'It was all a long time ago. I told you on the phone. I learned to think before I act. Prison is a great teacher.'

He lifted one finger to follow the line of that

narrow scar bisecting his cheek. 'I thought I was tough as a kid but I had a lot to learn.'

Ella's heart lurched. Imagine going behind bars as a teenager and emerging a man. Imagine who he'd mixed with there. No wonder Donato had a hard, impenetrable edge.

That scar, though silvered now, scored perilously close to the corner of his eye. It was faint enough to give him a rakish hint of the buccaneer, but she'd dealt with knife wounds when she'd worked in Emergency. She knew what sliced flesh looked like.

'Ella?' His breath feathered her face, warm and coffee-scented. 'You're feeling *sorry* for me?' His brows knitted as he leaned over her, astonishment clear in those brilliant eyes.

'No, I…'

Her words dissolved as his lips brushed hers, soft and almost tentative.

That was all it took. One kiss. Not even a kiss but the merest whisper of a caress, and she ignited, falling against him as he tugged her in. He wrapped his arms around her, not hard, but to her disordered mind it seemed protectively, tenderly. That just fuelled her response, like petrol poured on open flames.

He pulled his head back to stare down at her, his gaze darkening to midnight.

'I don't need your pity.' She felt the rumble of his voice through their bodies, where she pressed against him. 'I was found guilty, remember?'

'Who said anything about pity?' Yet there was a knot in her throat at the idea of him as a kid, coming of age in prison because he'd tried to defend someone.

His look sharpened. 'Women want me because I'm rich. Because I'm powerful. Or for a thrill because I'm big and bad and dangerous.' That unblinking gaze pinioned her. '*Never* because they feel sorry for me.'

It was a warning, as clear as a flashing red light. Yet he hadn't mentioned the most obvious reason any woman would want him. Because he was the single most fascinating, sexy, infuriatingly charismatic man on the planet.

Ella had finally found a weak spot in his aura of omniscient authority. When she had more time, when she wasn't pressed up against him from thigh to breast, she'd think about that.

Now, though, her thoughts frayed. Logical Ella was unravelling. That new bold Ella stirred again, the woman who dared to act on impulse, regardless of consequences. She shuddered as desire rose like a blast of hot summer air.

'Good, then you won't expect sentiment from me.' She rose on her toes and anchored her hands in his thick soft hair, pulling him down to her level.

She was confused by this man, alternately irritated and fascinated. But she *needed* him. More now than before, as if what they'd shared earlier had given her a taste of something deliciously addictive.

'Kiss me, Donato.' It was new Ella speaking, her voice an unfamiliar throaty purr. 'And make it good.'

Ella had never said anything like that to a man. But the fingers threading his hair were hers, as were the breasts straining against his hard torso, and the hips circling needily as he clamped her against him. The mouth was definitely hers, fusing with his demanding lips, sighing her pleasure as he forgot about conversation and gave her what she needed.

By the time they made it to a large canopied day bed near the pool, she was in her underwear and he'd lost his shirt and shoes.

Ella lay back, enjoying the view of his bronzed

torso, powerful and dusted with dark hair across the chest. Even the couple of scars, pale on his ribs, didn't mar his perfection. Muscles bunched and twisted as he reached for a condom then shoved down his pants.

A gasp escaped and he looked up.

It would be too naïve of her to blurt out that he was the most imposing man she'd ever seen. Just the sight of him made her heart hammer.

'You're well prepared.' Was that her voice, that husky drawl of invitation? 'Do you usually carry so many condoms?'

His mouth curved in a tight smile at odds with the blaze in his eyes. 'I was expecting you.'

He reached out, dispensing with her underwear with casual efficiency. His eyes like lasers, so hot she felt her skin shiver. Then his mouth was on her breast, his hand between her legs, and there was nothing but Donato and pleasure so intense it saturated her, from her bones to her brain and everywhere in between.

He licked her nipple and her breath caught. He sucked it inside his hot mouth and her hands on the back of his head turned to claws, dragging him closer.

His hand moved and she bucked against him. Impossibly she felt a trembling begin deep inside. A trembling that grew and spread.

'Now! I need you now.' Desperately she groped down between them. He was thick and solid against her palm, twitching at her touch.

Heat suffused her, intensified at the slide of his hard body against hers. The tickle of chest hair against her breasts, the haze of his breath on her neck. His fingers covered hers, guiding, till he was right where she needed him.

Their eyes locked as Donato dragged her hands above her head, holding them high against the cushions as he thrust home with one hungry glide that brought them colliding together.

Ella arched up, stunned by the sheer intimacy of him there, at the heart of her, his eyes holding hers as surely as he claimed her body. The air locked in her lungs as sensation rocked her. Not physical sensation but something she couldn't name, a sense of rightness, of belonging.

Donato's eyes widened. Did he feel it too?

Ella remembered how it had felt coming apart in his arms, drowning in his gaze. She felt it again, fierce pleasure and more too, the powerful connection, the sense she gave up part of her soul, not just her body. It had scared the life out of her.

She squeezed her eyes shut, focusing on the crescendo of physical rapture. The climax that was upon her before she knew it, throwing her high to the stars. She bit her tongue, desperate not to cry his name as ecstasy took over, needing not to give in completely.

Donato jerked hard, spilling himself, his voice a guttural, seductive slur of Spanish, and her eyes opened of their own volition.

Instantly she was lost in indigo heat, in the heady, terrifying tumble into unfamiliar territory that wasn't merely about eager bodies and erotic caresses. Into a place where she was no longer Ella but part of him, part of Donato, and he was part of her.

He held her gaze for what seemed minutes, their breathing ragged, chests heaving, bodies twitching in the aftershock of that momentous eruption of delight.

Ella told herself it was okay. She'd be fine. She was just unused to sex. To giving herself to any man. This was purely physical.

Then he bent his head and touched his lips to hers in a delicate feather of a kiss and something huge and inexplicable welled up inside. Ella choked back a lump in her throat, blinking furiously as heat glazed her eyes and a tear spilled down her cheek.

CHAPTER NINE

'IF YOU STAY the night, who knows,' Donato murmured hours later, languidly tracing Ella's back, 'we might make it to a bed.'

It was the first time he'd invited a woman to stay overnight but he'd passed the stage of being surprised at his need for Ella. Whatever this was between them, he'd enjoy it to the utmost.

A rich chuckle shivered through her, tickling his hand and tugging at something in his belly. She had a warm, sexy laugh. 'That would be a novelty.'

He smiled. That was better. The sight of her silver eyes awash with tears had disturbed him, even if it had been in the aftermath of a stunning climax.

He'd gathered her close, ignoring the upsurge of desire as she settled across him. The shadows had lengthened and she'd slept, making him wonder at her exhaustion. Perhaps she hadn't slept last night either.

Ella Sanderson wasn't what he'd expected. From her plain cotton bra and knickers, as if she'd deliberately dressed *not* to entice him, to the look in her eyes when she'd probed about his past.

Donato's chest clenched. No one since his mother had ever been completely on his side, not even his lawyer. He wasn't used to it. That explained the weird, full sensation when Ella had looked at him with such sympathy, her mouth a pout of distress.

He shook off a sense of disquiet. Deliberately he pulled her against his erection, enjoying her gasp. He enjoyed holding a woman who was all sweet curves and hollows. He looked forward to exploring every centimetre.

A phone pierced the silence and Ella moved. Donato was surprised at the strength of his urge to tug her back.

'That's mine.' She scrambled across the day bed, breasts swaying, her peach of a backside making his mouth dry as he imagined taking her from behind.

'It can wait.' He propped himself on one elbow for a better view. How could a woman who looked as good as Ella doubt her attractiveness? He'd put the pieces together now—her discomfort when he'd called her attractive, her haughtiness that defied him to find fault and the surprise in her silvery eyes when he'd pulled back to admire her.

'It might be important.' She scooped up her phone and, before he could stop her, stood.

'On a Saturday?' What could be so vital? Another lover? The idea punched his gut. Instinct, or maybe pride, told him Ella wasn't promiscuous, despite the rampant sex they'd shared. He'd seen her shock when they came together so spectacularly and her dazed disbelief when rapture claimed her.

He guessed her bravado hid a deep reserve.

His gaze lingered on her hourglass figure, slightly broader at the hips and deliciously narrow at the waist. Long shapely legs and hair like dark honey. She wrapped a nearby towel around herself and scowled at the phone.

'Hello, Dad.' Her voice was wary. More than wary.

Donato's interest stirred.

Ella shot a harried glance at him then moved away. But the curve of the building improved the acoustics so he caught part of the conversation.

'No, it's not all settled! We'll find another way.' She hunched the phone against her ear and pulled back her shoulder-length hair in a gesture that screamed frustration.

'You wouldn't! That's Rob's money. You have to repay that before you do anything else.' Another look over her shoulder before she walked to the end of the pool.

Donato watched her long-legged stride. She couldn't keep still. One hand slashed the air and her mouth turned down as if she'd swallowed something sour.

Talking to Reg Sanderson had that effect on him too.

So there was a rift between father and daughter. He'd guessed that, seeing the lack of affection between them. Plus there was outrage in Ella's voice when she spoke of Rob's money. Rob, her brother? Had Sanderson got his claws into his kids' assets?

Donato shouldn't have promised not to investigate her and, by extension, her siblings. It tied his hands. There was far more he wanted to know, but having given her his word—

She strode back, her features taut. Something clenched hard inside him.

'Come here.' Donato put out his hand. 'You need someone to help you feel better. I'm just the man.'

His invitation wasn't entirely selfish. He didn't

like her troubled expression, knowing Sanderson had caused it. Another reason to hate the man.

Ella lifted her hand as if to take his, then stopped. 'No.' Her hand dropped and Donato was surprised at the strength of his disappointment. 'Thank you. But…' She shook her head and the afternoon sun caught the sheen of honey gilt. 'I need to go.'

Donato was about to insist she remain when he read the strain around her mouth. He knew he could have her in his bed all night, enjoying what his body urged him to take. He could weasel the information he wanted after breaking down her defences.

He let his arm fall. He wanted Ella's passion and her sweet body. He wanted to understand her and her relationship with her father. But he wouldn't seduce the details from her.

His belly churned in a moment of unfamiliar disquiet. He was already taking advantage, pretending to want marriage. It wasn't just Sanderson pressuring her, putting the shadows beneath her bright eyes.

Amazingly, for the first time in years, doubt shivered through what passed for his conscience. More than doubt, it was guilt, its sharp blade scraping.

Donato sat up, his jaw setting as Ella gathered

her clothes. She might be vulnerable and sassy, sexy and funny and, he suspected, brave, but he couldn't allow her to stand in the way of justice.

Nothing would save Reg Sanderson from his deserts. Not even the fact his daughter was the most appealing, fascinating woman Donato could recall knowing.

He stood, retrieving her floaty top that had landed on the day bed's high canopy.

'Thank you.' Her eyes didn't meet his and he caught again that hint of embarrassment.

Their hands brushed and sensation jolted. *Maldición!* Need was like an electric current running through him.

'I'll see you tomorrow.'

She shook her head and he had to restrain himself from catching those honey-brown tresses and hauling her close again.

'I'm busy.'

'Be ready at nine. I'll collect you.'

'You don't know where I live. And you promised not to set your investigators onto me.'

Donato suppressed a smile. That was better. Her eyes shone with challenge and her chin notched high.

'I didn't promise not to follow you home.' He

let that sink in. 'I'll just toss on some clothes.' He reached for his shirt, absently noting a couple of missing buttons.

Her deep sigh drew his attention. Despite her defiant air, she clutched her clothes close, hiding herself. As if he couldn't perfectly recall those enticing curves.

'Okay. I'll meet you tomorrow. I'll come here at midday.'

'Nine.'

'Eleven.'

'Nine.' He brushed her hair off her cheek. 'And I promise not to ring you after midnight.' She shivered and he moved closer, inhaling her skin's delicate perfume, like sweet peas and sunshine.

'Nine-thirty, then. And you won't call me at all.'

Donato didn't say anything. If she thought he'd pass up a chance to hear her voice, husky and delicious, when he couldn't have her in his bed…well, she didn't know him yet.

'That's it. You've got the hang of it now.' Donato's voice was warm with approval and encouragement and Ella felt emotion flare. Pleasure? Pride? Or excitement at being so close to him?

No time to work it out now. She had to concentrate.

'Shift your left hand.'

She watched as Donato demonstrated. Like her, he was suspended on a rope, halfway down a rock face. Except, unlike her, he was perfectly at ease. His eyes danced with pleasure and she'd seen his exhilaration earlier as he'd abseiled down the cliff then swarmed back up with an efficiency that left her in breathless awe.

She knew he was strong. It was two weeks since she'd become intimately acquainted with his body. But seeing him now she realised how carefully he leashed that power when they made love.

'Ella? Are you okay?'

'Fine.' She wrenched her gaze to the rock and made herself concentrate on his instructions. Carefully she stepped backwards, feeling the rope play out in her gloved hand.

'Perfect. You've got it.'

Delight filled her. It was partly the thrill of abseiling and partly the effect of his approval.

Since when had she wanted Donato's approval?

She froze, her throat catching.

'You're doing well, Ella. Just keep moving.' His voice was encouraging but businesslike enough to focus her. The perfect teacher.

Who'd have thought it? She remembered that

first night when he'd seemed so daunting with his saturnine looks and air of despotic authority.

But the Donato she'd begun to know had surprising depths. He got his own way too much and there was a shut-off side to him she couldn't penetrate, yet he was unexpectedly thoughtful and…kind.

He moved close but not close enough to crowd her. 'Try bending your knees and pushing off. Just a little bounce. You know you're safe.'

Ella nodded. She'd inspected the equipment, learning all she could before she'd agreed to try this. And their professional guide was at the top, watching out for her.

Tentatively she bent her legs, pushing off from the rock. For a dizzying instant fear hit her, then the thrill of it kicked in. She did it again, this time releasing the rope a little so she moved out and down in an arc.

'I did it!' A grin split her face.

'Of course you did, since you set your mind to it.'

Ella turned and found Donato smiling as if he was as thrilled as she was. The warmth of his smile lit her inside.

'Come on, let's get to the bottom.'

Ella turned back to the rock, concentrating on each movement. Yet as she descended, thrilled by the fun of it, she was aware of him beside her, matching his pace to hers.

Finally she stood on shaky legs, breathing hard, adrenalin coursing through her body.

'Good?' Donato pulled her close, his hands on her hips, and a different sort of thrill shot through her.

'Marvellous.'

'Glad you agreed to try something different this weekend?'

'Absolutely.' She braced her hands on his shoulders when he would have pulled her closer. 'When did you learn to climb?'

He waited before replying, as if assessing her curiosity. 'In my early twenties. I discovered a taste for wide-open spaces.' His mouth curled at the corner. 'Not surprising after being penned in. When I could, which wasn't often, given I was building a business from scratch, I'd get out of the city. Windsurfing, climbing, hang-gliding.'

'They sound challenging.' And dangerous.

'I like the wind in my hair. The feeling of not being hemmed in.'

Ella thought of his Sydney house. Set at the top of a cliff with a commanding view of the Pacific, it was as un-hemmed-in as you could get in such a metropolis.

'What about you, Ella?' He tilted up her chin so his words brushed her face. 'What do you do to unwind?'

Make love with a breathtakingly gorgeous, enigmatic tycoon.

This fortnight there'd been no time for anything but work and Donato. If she wasn't with him in the evening, he was flirting with her over the phone, his espresso-dark voice a constant reminder of what she missed by refusing to stay with him.

But the need to keep part of her life private remained strong. Donato had stormed into her world like a cyclone flattening every defence. He dominated her thoughts and even her dreams.

'How do I unwind? You'll find out soon enough.' Their weekend in the Blue Mountains west of the city was in two parts. Donato had suggested they spend half the time doing something he enjoyed and the other half was her choice.

As if he wanted to share his private life with her, not just his bed. As if he wanted to know more about her too. It was a beguiling idea. After two weeks of toe-curling orgasms and carefully light banter, this signalled a shift in their relationship.

Ella had tried telling herself they didn't have a relationship. They had sex. Stunning, all-eclipsing sex.

And they had this farcical engagement. Her father insisted they were marrying and went ahead with preparations despite her protests. But it would take more than his demands to make her marry a man she didn't love.

Meanwhile she needed to help her siblings. Her father had misappropriated Rob's inheritance from their grandfather, the money he needed to finish the resort's refurbishment. Reg had promised to repay it when his business with Donato was sorted.

Ella felt trapped, by her attraction to Donato and the situation with her father.

She'd told Donato repeatedly there'd be no wedding. Every time he'd shrugged and said it would all work out.

It was like a game, one where only he knew the rules. When she tried to press for a resolution he distracted her, usually with some outrageous provocation that led to verbal sparring and, most often, sex.

Now he wrapped his arms around her and her heart gave a familiar leap. 'Don't I get a kiss for introducing you to abseiling?'

She shook her head, teasing. 'It was our guide who did the work, organising the equipment and—'

'If you think you're kissing anyone but me,' Donato growled, a light in his eyes, 'you're sadly mistaken.'

Instantly she was all quivering anticipation. That hint of possessiveness was too appealing.

She wanted Donato. Not just his kisses but his attention, his time. Warning bells clanged.

Ella needed to remind him, and herself, she was her own woman. He was so overwhelming it was a constant battle not to be swept up, simply giving in to him.

She put a hand on Donato's broad chest, pushing. 'That's for me to choose. You don't *own* me, Donato. You haven't bought me.'

She'd anticipated a mock scowl, or that lethally slow smile that stirred all her senses.

What she got was sudden stillness and a look that made the hairs on her nape stand on end. Not a look of anger. She couldn't read his expression, but she knew he'd gone somewhere she didn't want to be.

His hold tightened, his fingers digging too hard. Then suddenly she was free. Donato stepped back, hands flexing. His chest rose as he sucked oxygen, like a swimmer too long underwater.

'Donato? What is it?' His stark expression made the blood curdle in her veins. Shivers ran down her arms and disquiet stirred.

His eyes were fixed on the distance.

'Donato?'

His gaze swung down to her. She read turmoil and strong emotion. What was going on? One minute he was laughing and intimate. The next he'd totally withdrawn.

'Of course.' The last vestiges of tension vanished as she watched. He looked the same as ever, confident and in control. But Ella knew something had happened, as it had when he'd spoken of his past.

What was he hiding? Everyone had secrets, but she sensed Donato's cast very long shadows.

Ella gripped his arms, needing the physical connection. Needing, if possible, to help. His taut biceps were hard as the rock they'd just traversed. She loved his strength. Being with Donato made her feel almost petite and dainty.

Deliberately she stood on her toes and brushed her mouth against his. Instantly he responded with a slow, bone-melting thoroughness that made her wish their guide wasn't waiting above.

Finally Donato pulled back.

'Come on, Ella. It's time you learned how to climb back up.' His lips curled in that devastating smile and she found herself smiling back.

But she was silent as he busied himself with their gear. For his smile had been wrong. It hadn't reached his eyes.

Ella told herself that just because they were lovers didn't give her the right to pry into things he obviously didn't want to share. She too kept part of her life off-limits to Donato.

Yet the need to understand him gnawed. She wanted to know so she could help. Because she never wanted to see that blank shadow on his face again.

Was that the reaction of a short-term lover?

Or was it the reaction of a woman sinking deep over her head?

CHAPTER TEN

'RETAIL THERAPY!' Donato groaned. 'I knew it was a mistake to let you choose our activity for the day.'

Yet it was a token protest. After spending a whole night with Ella, waking with her in his arms for the first time, it would take more than a little shopping to spoil his mood.

Last night, after their day of climbing and abseiling, there'd been an intensity to her passion he couldn't get enough of. Given their history of instant attraction and explosive loving, that was saying something.

The sooner she moved in with him the better.

Donato ignored the voice reminding him he'd never shared his home with any woman.

This was different. Ella wasn't a clinging vine, grasping for the material things he could provide.

Hard to believe that she was Sanderson's daughter. The more he knew her, the less like her father she was.

'If you haven't got the stamina for it, Donato, go back to the hotel.' She flashed him a look of pure challenge.

'Stamina?' He stared down into those stunning eyes with mock indignation. 'I defy you to find a man with more stamina.'

For a moment Ella's eyes looked more pewter than blue, just like when she lost herself in his arms. Instantly his heart beat faster.

'We'll see how you fare after a few hours hunting for lost treasure.' Then she turned to bend over an ancient moth-eaten chair, dismissing him.

Donato smiled. Perversely, he loved the fact Ella made a point of not kowtowing to him. For years, since his phenomenal burst of commercial success, people had fallen over themselves to agree with him. No one dismissed him.

He liked that Ella treated him like an ordinary man. Neither a commercially astute businessman whose every pronouncement was gold, nor a sinister outsider to polite society who could never be completely trusted because of his murky past.

And he liked knowing that no matter how pointedly she stood up to him, he just had to touch her and she went up in flames.

'Treasure? Hunting through junk, don't you mean?'

She shrugged. 'If you can't cope I'll see you later.'

But Donato wasn't going anywhere. He was fascinated, watching Ella's assessing eye as she prowled the antiques centre. He'd developed an interest in antiques himself, drawn by the idea of a bygone world of grace and beauty that was everything his early life hadn't been.

Ella moved through the place, her sharp eyes spotting the same mantel clock he did. It belonged not in a dusty bric-a-brac emporium, but in a collector's home. Then she paused by a tiny damaged table. He hadn't noticed it. Now he realised how finely it was made. With restoration it would be beautiful.

Ella had a good eye. It intrigued him to think they shared an interest in beautiful old things.

But what kept him at her side, helping her shift a lumpy chair to get to an old trunk, was more than an interest in antiques. She almost hummed with happiness as she explored. Her enthusiasm drew him.

She was appealing when she challenged him, standing so haughtily, refusing to cave in despite her father's pushing. But when she was happy…

Donato was surprised at the cliché that sprang to mind. But it was true. When Ella was happy she *glowed.*

He wanted to bask in that radiance. Her lips curved in an excited smile as she ran her hands over the trunk. Donato wanted to be part of what made her happy. He wanted to make her smile.

How long since he'd wanted to do that for anyone?

It was a relief to see her like this. Yesterday, with a few casual words, she'd unleashed a wave of bitter remembrance. More than that, she'd evoked guilt.

You don't own me.

You haven't bought me.

Even now his blood iced at the words. At the implication he was stripping away her control of her own life by agreeing to this sham engagement.

Did she really feel disempowered?

Acid swirled in his belly and rose, filling his mouth.

His fight wasn't with Ella. It was with her father. He'd imagined Sanderson's daughter would be as shallow and selfish as him, eager to triumph in the role of high-profile fiancée to a rich entrepreneur.

Instead he'd found a woman whose idea of a good time was hunting for old wares.

You haven't bought me.

Donato's jaw clamped so hard pain radiated through his skull.

He knew, exactly, what it meant to buy someone. To own someone.

The words, so casual, so meaningless to most, were honed knives. They sliced into the darkness that was his past and his very essence. He felt the ice-hot slash, not to his face or his ribs this time, but to his heart. It heaved as the blackness of the past rose up.

'Donato.' A hand touched his and he looked down. Ella's eyes met his. Stunned, he felt again that spark of connection he'd told himself he'd imagined. This time it was a welcome sizzle of heat, cracking the ice in his veins. 'Come and look at this.'

Did she know? Had she seen the murky shadows engulf him?

Donato straightened. Of course she hadn't. No one did. They were his to bear alone.

'What have you found now? Jewellery?' He forced a smile to his face and watched her blink. That was better. He preferred Ella distracted rather than questioning. 'It has to be something glittery to make a woman so excited.'

'Don't pretend to be a sexist beast. We both know you're not.'

'Not sexist?'

Their gazes locked and, extraordinarily, Donato felt as if her assessing gaze saw too much. 'Not either.'

Which showed how little Ella knew about him.

Because of his prison record most women viewed him with trepidation, even if mingled with a good dollop of excitement. They fantasised about the bad boy, especially one who had wealth to smooth his way. If they knew the full details of his past they'd shun him. That had never mattered. He didn't care about the approval of pampered society women.

Yet with Ella, for the first time, he almost wished he were a different man. Except that would mean denying his past and he would never do that.

She linked her fingers with his and tugged. Donato was surprised at how good that felt. 'Come on. I want your opinion on this. It reminds me of something you have in that mansion of yours.'

Despite his teasing grumbles, Donato was good company. Better company than Ella had expected.

This was the second day they'd spent together doing something other than fall into bed. Not that they'd ever needed a bed. Heat danced through Ella's veins. It had taken two visits to Donato's house to make it as far as his bedroom. Even then they hadn't made it to the mattress.

When he'd suggested a weekend together she'd thought they'd be naked. Instead she'd found something even more distracting.

A man who switched off his phone to spend time in the wilderness, introducing her to some of the extreme sports he enjoyed.

A man with patience and humour, who took time to ensure she enjoyed herself.

Donato didn't care about keeping up appearances like her father. All morning he'd helped her fossick amongst collectables and downright junk. He hadn't blinked when he'd got dust on those exquisite casual clothes or she'd asked him to heave furniture out of the way.

Ella wondered what he'd make of her choice for the afternoon. She led him through the gate of the National Trust property and into the garden.

'More antiques?' He looked around with interest.

'You haven't been here?'

'I'm from Melbourne, remember.'

Ella felt a fillip of pleasure at introducing him to one of her favourite places.

'It's a heritage house and garden.' Said like that it sounded boring and she'd thought hard about bringing Donato here.

But the Everglades was special. When she'd first visited she'd been young enough to wonder if there were fairies in the wide sweep of bluebells that clustered here in spring. Later she'd been enchanted by the peace and beauty of the rambling gardens. After the fraught atmosphere at home, this had seemed like Paradise.

'You'll enjoy the house. I know you like art deco.'

'I sense a theme. It seems a favourite of yours too.' Ella heard his smile but didn't look up. Already she spent too much time under Donato's spell.

Ella shrugged. 'My mother's aunt lived in a nineteen-thirties house. I loved it.' Actually, she'd loved the peace and sense of acceptance, so different from her own home. Eventually that had translated into an appreciation of the house and its style.

Her great-aunt had brought Ella on trips here. She hadn't worried that her niece preferred to celebrate her birthday quietly instead of at a catered party for a hundred. Ella's father had thought her mad. Aunt Bea had encouraged her.

'She was important to you.'

Ella swung round. 'How did you know?'

'You sounded wistful.' His fingers brushed her cheek in a gesture that felt alarmingly tender. Ella was used to passion or provocation. Tenderness was usually reserved for the bedroom.

But this weekend there'd been more. His expression made her throat tighten.

'She *was* important,' Ella said eventually. 'My mother died when I was young and Aunt Bea was…special.' Ella had felt closer to the old lady than to her father. It didn't matter if Ella had puppy fat or a boring penchant for books. Or that she didn't sparkle in company. Aunt Bea had loved her, and through her Ella had learned to respect herself. 'She brought me here.'

'In that case I'm glad you chose to share it with me.' He threaded his fingers through hers in a gesture that seemed as intimate as the sex they'd shared this morning. Her tight throat constricted further.

Ella reminded herself that Donato was clever and perceptive. It was obvious the place was important to her.

Yet not even logic shattered the sensation of closeness, of *understanding.*

As if she understood Donato! He still wouldn't stop her father's nonsense about a wedding.

'Come on, there's a lot to see.' Ella stepped forward, under the spreading boughs of the ornamental trees. But she didn't shake off Donato's grip. There was something comfortable about simply holding hands, something…appealing.

They explored the garden theatre, the landscaped terraces and the lookout across the cliffs to the wilderness beyond. It was as they meandered back, past the house and a section where plants were being propagated, that she noticed Donato's abstraction.

He paused, surveying a bed of freshly turned soil and tiny plants. To Ella's inexperienced eye the scene wasn't as interesting as the rest of the grounds.

'Are you a gardener?' Why hadn't she thought of that? She'd been explaining what she knew of the garden design. Maybe he knew more than her, given his choice to live in a home with beautiful grounds rather than an easy-care apartment. 'You should have stopped me. It didn't occur to me—'

'I'm no expert,' he said, eyes still fixed on the garden bed. 'It just reminded me of something.'

'Really?' Ella moved closer. 'What does it remind you of?'

'Smell that? Fresh turned soil and compost.'

Ella inhaled. 'It's…earthy.'

'Good, rich soil. Someone has put in a lot of effort here.'

'What does it remind you of?'

He bent to pluck a couple of tiny weeds out of the carefully tended bed. 'When I was a kid we had a big vegetable garden. It smelled like this. Of earth and growing things.'

He straightened and turned, moving briskly away. Ella hastened after him. 'You enjoyed gardening?' It was the first glimpse he'd given of his past except for the few bare answers to her probing about his prison sentence.

Donato shrugged. 'It was a chore, that's all.'

Yet he'd taken time to pull out the weeds amongst the tiny seedlings. 'You didn't like it?'

Again that lift of broad shoulders. 'It had to be done. It supplied a lot of our food.'

'Whose garden was it? Your mother's or your father's?' Ella knew nothing about his family and suddenly the need to know more about him was overwhelming.

'You're curious all of a sudden.'

'Why not? You've got nothing to hide, have you?'

Donato stopped beneath the shade of an overhanging tree. 'Everyone has something to hide.' In the relative gloom he looked bigger than ever, his broad chest and shoulders imposing. But it was his voice that sent a ripple of warning through her. There was steel in that tone, telling her she'd trespassed too far.

This from the man who'd upended her calm, orderly life! So much for believing they'd begun to build something new this weekend.

'You're scared to tell me even that?' She shook her head. 'Is it so secret?'

He folded his arms. It made him look more impressively masculine and annoyingly attractive.

'Says the woman who refuses to mention she works in case I find out too much about her.' At her stare he nodded. 'Of course I know. You're never available during the week before six at night. I may be busy with my own business but I notice these things.'

Heat rushed up Ella's throat and into her cheeks. He was right. She'd avoided talking about herself, except at the most superficial level—food, music, books, sex. Nothing about her family or career. Nothing emotionally intimate. Until today when she'd told him about Aunt Bea. It had seemed such a huge concession—revealing even that tiny snippet.

She'd understood from the first that Donato was dangerous. Instinct had warned not to let him close. When she'd been unable to resist him physically, she'd worked to isolate him from the rest of her life. He didn't even know where she lived.

But he'd been no more forthcoming. She refused to feel guilty.

'I hardly think talking about your childhood chores constitutes an invasion of privacy.' She crossed her arms, imitating his challenging stance. All it got her was a heavy-lidded glance at her plumped-up breasts that sent traceries of fire through her belly.

Ella's instantaneous response to Donato was so predictable and so profound it unnerved her. She was torn between wanting more and wanting nothing to do with him. Because above all she wanted to discover what made him tick.

With a huff of self-disgust Ella spun away. The game he played was too deep. She'd begun to believe they shared something more profound than incendiary sex. Clearly she'd fooled herself.

'Wait!' A hand on her arm halted her.

Ella looked at his fingers loosely circling her flesh. Even that was enough to send a zing of anticipation through her. Her body had never got the message that Donato wasn't to be trusted.

'I'll make a deal with you.' His hand slid up her arm in a caress. She swallowed. She wouldn't let him seduce her again. 'I'll answer your question if you answer one of mine. Truthfully.'

'I don't lie.' She drew herself up.

'But there are things you'd rather not discuss.'

He was going to ask about her father and his business. It had to be that because that was Donato's real focus, the reason he'd taken an interest in her.

Hurt blossomed. But Ella was a big girl. She could cope. She could juggle the need to protect her family and her attraction to Donato.

Still holding her arm, he moved to lean back against the trunk of a massive tree. Before she could protest he pulled her against him, his arms wrapped around her waist from behind, her bottom tucked between his legs.

'No, don't move.' His voice was a soft burr, feathering her ear. 'Just relax.'

Being held felt so good, the solidity of Donato's body at her back, his arms holding her. Ella gave up and let her head sink against his collarbone. She stared out at the greenery screening them from the rest of the garden.

'The garden didn't belong to my mother,' Donato said. 'She knew as little about growing things as I did. It was Jack's.'

'Your father's?'

Donato didn't move. His heart beat steadily behind her. Yet something stirred—a change in his breathing? A feeling of wariness?

'I didn't know my father. Jack became my mother's partner when I was six.'

'Your stepfather then.'

Donato slid his fingers through hers and stroked the palm of her hand. 'No. He never thought of himself as my stepfather.'

Ella frowned. There was something so…guarded about the way he spoke.

Of course there was! He was the most self-contained person she knew. Yet something niggled. She'd expected more warmth in his voice over a childhood reminiscence. But then, most of her childhood memories were less than happy. Had it been like that for Donato too?

'He was abusive?'

'Jack was decent in his own way. He just wasn't interested in kids. All he cared about was my mother.' *Now* there was a shift in his voice, a depth of feeling he didn't bother to hide. 'He put me to work as soon as we moved in with him—set me to weeding while he began extending the vegetable patch since it had to feed three instead of one.'

A muffled laugh rumbled up from behind her. She felt as well as heard it.

'What's so funny?' Being dependent on the food you grew was no laughing matter.

'I was determined to do a good job, impress him so he wouldn't kick us out. By the time he'd turned back to check on me I'd ripped out half his precious seedlings and he treated me to some curses even I hadn't heard before.'

Ella watched a pair of crimson rosellas land in the tree before them, quietly chattering. But her thoughts were on Donato at six, convinced he had to work hard so as not to be kicked out. A child surprised to hear swearing that was new. What sort of life had he led?

Her hands tightened on his. 'Is that all he did?'

'He made me replant everything I'd pulled out. Then he gave us both a lesson in plant recognition. Neither of us knew a tomato plant from a potato or a bean.'

'So your mother was city bred too?'

'That's more than one question.' He sounded relaxed but, pressed against him, Ella felt the infinitesimal tightening of his muscles. 'It's my turn.'

'Okay.' She braced herself for a probing question about her father's business or ethics. That was what he'd want to know. That was why he'd demanded honesty.

'Tell me about your job.'

'Sorry?' She turned her head but the curve of his shoulder and encircling arm stopped her seeing his face.

'I want to know what work you do. It's no use pretending you're like your sister, living off Daddy's money and drifting from one amusement to another.'

'I never implied I did!'

'I asked upfront how important your father's money was to you—whether it supported you—and you didn't correct me.'

Ella remembered that conversation the night they'd met. She'd been out of her depth, fighting not to show it. She'd been furious and combative. Later she'd revealed as little as possible about her life. It was her only defence against the feeling Donato was taking over her world.

'I'm a nurse.'

'Ah.' His slow exhalation of breath stirred her hair. 'Now, why doesn't that surprise me?'

Here it comes. She'd heard it all from her father. Everything from the dowdy uniform to the unglamorous nature of the job and the low pay.

'I have no idea. But I'm sure you're going to tell me.' Ella tried to pull away, but Donato's seemingly lazy hold kept her hard against him.

'Now, Ella, there's no need to get annoyed.' His lips brushed her hair. 'I hadn't guessed but it makes sense.'

'Do tell.' She gritted her teeth. In her family circle, nurses didn't exist. Careers were high profile or highly paid, preferably both. Emptying bedpans or cleaning wounds was just too nose-wrinklingly real.

'You're so assured. Nothing fazes you.' He stroked a finger along one bare arm, drawing her skin into feathery lines of goose bumps. 'You get angry and you're deeply passionate, but I can't imagine you panicking.'

'Assured?' Ella stared at the bright birds in the tree as if she'd never seen them before. She was competent and confident in her work but she didn't feel assured with Donato. He kept her off balance.

A chuckle rose in his deep chest and vibrated through her. 'Absolutely. You put me in my place from the first. But you weren't patronising in that socially superior way. You weren't a snob. You just said it like it was.'

'I'm practical.' Her father had used that word like an insult.

'Just like every nurse I've met.'

'You've met a few?' She thought of that old scar on his cheek and the others on his ribs.

'Enough. You've got that same air of straight talking, but with all the aplomb of a duchess.' It didn't sound like criticism. It sounded like a compliment. Ella felt a little fizz of pleasure.

'Have you ever met a duchess?'

'I have, as it happens. She was more pleasant and down-to-earth than some of the snobby society types I've met.'

'I can imagine.' Her father was one such snob.

He'd forgive you anything so long as you were rich or socially superior.

'So, what sort of nursing?' Donato sounded genuinely interested.

'Community care. I visit people in their homes, often the elderly or patients just released from hospital.'

'In their homes? Do you work in pairs?'

'I'm part of a team but I do my home visits solo.'

Donato's arms tightened. 'That's dangerous. You don't know what you could walk into.'

'We're fully trained. We have safety protocols in place. Anyway, most of my clients are frail.'

'It's not just your clients. *Anyone* could be there.'

'I can look after myself, Donato.' She turned in his arms and pressed a finger to his mouth before he could contradict her. 'But I appreciate your concern.'

In all her years of nursing none of her family or friends had expressed concern for her safety. That must explain the strange melting sensation in her chest as she met his stare. She'd never had a protector. There'd been no one since her mother or Aunt Bea who worried about her. Fuzz and Rob saw her as capable and efficient, able to look after herself. And their father…he'd never cared enough to worry.

Crazy that the man logic told her not to trust was the one man who worried about her.

Crazier still that she liked it.

CHAPTER ELEVEN

'WELL, YOU COULD have knocked me down with a feather. Really!' Samantha Raybourne's laugh tinkled melodiously, turning heads in the packed theatre lounge. 'I'd never thought of *you* marrying, Ella. Much less snaffling the most eligible man in the country.'

Ella's smile froze. Why had she told Donato she wanted to see this play? She should have known opening night would attract people like the dreadful Samantha, who'd once made her life hell. She hated that she'd put herself in this position, an unwilling partner in a public charade. But the constraints had been too great, despite her misgivings.

'What Sam means is congratulations.' Samantha's partner spoke. As compère of a reality television show he was adept at reading tension and knew when to intervene. 'We hope you'll both be very happy.'

Before Ella could respond Donato slipped his

arm around her waist. His grip reminded her, *as if she could forget*, of the promise he'd extracted. He'd keep her father from badgering her daily about arrangements for the society wedding he planned and in return Ella would play along in public. Even though it meant maintaining the fiction that their relationship was permanent.

A wave of stifling warmth enfolded her. She and Donato wouldn't really marry and it drove her crazy trying to work out why he let her father peddle such a fantasy. What had he to gain? Surely this wasn't the behaviour of an honest man. Yet everything she'd learned of Donato testified that he was straight down the line, often brutally so. His refusal to explain, and to stop the charade, was a dark blot on a relationship that was otherwise almost too enticing.

'Thanks for the good wishes.' Donato's deep rumble sliced through the chatter around them.

Ella was tempted to blurt out the truth, that the engagement was a lie. But Donato had warned that without the 'engagement' he'd stop all involvement with her father. That wasn't an option, not while her siblings needed Reg Sanderson to repay the money he'd taken.

She'd grown tired of trying to force the issue.

Whatever strange machinations went on between him and her father, ultimately neither could make her marry Donato. In the meantime she could only find relief in the fact that her real friends had no notion of the fake engagement. Only those in her father's set. Yet guilt and frustration gnawed at her.

'I had no idea the pair of you even knew each other,' Samantha purred, leaning forward to reveal even more pumped-up cleavage.

Anger pierced Ella. If she really were Donato's fiancée she'd take exception to the way the other woman pawed at him, chattering on about a party they'd both attended in Melbourne and giving him that intimate smile.

But Ella was just his temporary lover.

She hadn't let him encroach too far into her world. As for the time they spent on mutual interests, like antiques and art or activities new to her, like sailing and climbing, that didn't feel like encroachment. Those were pure pleasure.

In fact, she realised with a hitch to her breathing, *all* her time with Donato was pleasurable. Their sexual connection had grown into something more complex.

Ella blinked when Samantha leaned in and said with a saccharine smile, 'I get so bored when the men talk business, don't you? Media trends and market growth.' Beside them their companions were deep in discussion.

'No, I don't. I find it interesting.' When Donato spoke of his wide span of investments, she was fascinated.

'But then you've always been so serious, Ella. Serious and sturdy.' Samantha's violet eyes, their colour as artificial as her smile, swept Ella dismissively. 'That reminds me. Rumour has it your father's engaged Aurelio to design your wedding dress. Is it true?'

Ella shrugged, aiming for nonchalance despite her dismay. Surely her father hadn't gone as far as organising a dress and hiring the country's most exclusive designer! This was a nightmare. The sooner it ended the better.

Except when it ends you and Donato will go your separate ways.

Ella's stomach pinched. The thought of Donato moving on to another lover brought bile to her mouth.

She wanted what they had to last. She *enjoyed*

being with him. No one else had ever made her feel like this.

The revelation knocked her for six, making her sway.

Instantly Donato's arm tightened around her. He looked down, flashing her a reassuring smile before turning back to his conversation, and her stupid heart kicked up pace.

She wanted to be with him.

'I'm amazed you've got Aurelio to agree to design your gown.' Samantha had taken her silence for assent. 'His work is exquisite but he prefers to work with *petite* clients to show off his amazing designs.' Again that sharp gaze, dismissing Ella's body as unfashionably rounded.

'Rake-thin women, you mean?' Ella didn't bother pretending to misunderstand. 'I wouldn't know. I'm not really familiar with his designs.' She knew the name, of course, but that was all.

'You're not familiar…?' The other woman delicately fanned herself. 'But why would you when you're not the *type* he normally dresses.' Again that horrified survey of Ella's height and hips.

Ella told herself to be grateful for the woman's cattiness. It distracted her from dismay over the revelation of her feelings for Donato.

Yet Samantha's words opened old wounds. She'd always made Ella feel like a galumphing elephant, reinforcing all her father's negativity. She was too big, too serious and dull to be pretty or exciting.

'But then, Donato's a force to be reckoned with, isn't he? What are artistic scruples compared with the chance to dress his bride, no matter what her size?'

Donato felt the shift of supple muscle under his arm as Ella straightened. More than straightened. A ruler could lie exactly along her taut spine as she gazed down at the woman before her.

His skin tightened in a familiar flurry of anticipation as he felt energy radiate off Ella. From the first he'd enjoyed sparring with her.

Only this time her focus wasn't on him.

He watched Samantha What's-her-name wave a languid hand as she spoke in that awful arch tone about dresses and Ella's size.

Understanding hit and with it came fury. Red-hot fingers of rage dug into his chest, squeezing his lungs. His hand clamped so hard at Ella's waist she swung round, looking up questioningly.

Was it imagination or did her eyes look bruised? The idea disturbed him. Then as he watched something in her expression changed and her lips tilted up in a smile.

Only he saw that it didn't reach her eyes.

'I don't care what some dressmaker thinks of my body,' Ella said, her gaze holding his so that his pulse grew heavy. 'But Donato likes it.' She leaned towards him, flagrantly ignoring the other woman. 'Don't you, Nato?'

For a split second shock grabbed him, because she'd somehow chanced on the diminutive that only his mother had called him. Then a moment later came the stunned realisation that he liked the pet name on Ella's lips. He wanted to hear it again.

She blinked and he realised she was waiting for his response. Beyond her the hungry-looking woman with the blinding teeth and the bony collarbone watched avidly.

'You need to ask, *corazón*?' He let his hand slip down from the sweet incurve of Ella's waist to linger, circling at her hip. 'How could I look at another woman when I have you? You're the sexiest woman I know.'

'Even with my curves?' Her tinkle of laughter was a fair imitation of the woman standing before them, but Donato knew Ella well enough to hear the tightness in her voice. She did a good job of hiding it but, he realised, the other woman's words had struck home. He frowned, remembering so many times when Ella had tried to hide her body, as if uncomfortable with him seeing her naked.

'Your body,' he said deliberately, 'is a work of art.' He yanked her against him and her escaping breath puffed warm across his chin. 'Any designer would adore dressing you. You look like a woman, not a scrawny sack of bones.'

Dimly he was aware of a shocked hiss from the woman beside them, but his attention was on Ella's widening eyes.

Bending his head, he nipped the sensitive spot where her neck met her shoulder. She went limp, her head tipping back. Donato tasted summer fruit as he licked the spot then nuzzled his way up to her ear.

Ella gasped and clutched his shoulders and he scooped her closer, one hand at her hip, the other on the warm, smooth skin between her shoulder blades. Another kiss and she arched in silent invitation.

He needed to pull back. He'd made his point. They were in a public place.

But he didn't give a damn about creating a scene. Not with Ella in his arms. Not when he wanted to erase the hint of pain he'd read in her eyes. And forget the slash of guilt that he, with his insistence on this farce of an engagement, had made her a target for that witch's claws. But he couldn't renege now. Not so close to bringing Sanderson to ruin.

Did guilt heighten his desire? Donato wanted to lose himself in Ella. She was a drug in his blood, a pleasure he'd grown addicted to.

Carajo, he was even hearing bells now. Kissing Ella, holding her in his arms, made him forget where he was.

Her hands on his shoulders shifted, pushed, and she pulled her head back. Dazed silver eyes met his, their pupils huge and unfocused.

Donato leaned in to take her mouth again.

'No.' Her whisper came from lips now bare of make-up but deliciously dark and plump from their kisses. 'Interval's over.'

Donato looked around the rapidly emptying space. What had begun as a deliberate display had become something else. The burn of rage and guilt in his belly and the indefinable emotions that stirred when Ella had turned to him, looking proud yet so vulnerable, had torn away something within him. He'd wanted to erase every vestige of hurt from her face, but in the process he'd lost himself.

Nato, she'd called him. And it had felt right. So right he hadn't wanted to draw back.

He'd wanted to help her but he'd also needed to tap into that sense of well-being she always gave him. It was a feeling he'd come to crave.

And he'd wanted to possess her. Still he clutched her, one hand anchored now in her honey-brown hair, making a delectable mess of her upswept style.

She straightened, her hands going self-consciously to her hair as her gaze slid to the last stragglers.

'Leave it,' Donato growled, his voice rough. 'I prefer it that way.'

'And that's all that matters, is it?' She tossed her head, pouting, and he smiled.

'No, but it's true. And surely I deserve some reward.'

Her eyes narrowed. 'Because you lied about my body to save my pride.'

'You really have no idea, do you, *cariño*?' She was a remarkable mix of savvy and innocent. 'I spoke nothing but the truth.'

Her beautiful mouth sagged and he smiled wryly.

'I deserve a reward because, despite my inclinations, I'm going to take you in to see the second half of the play. I'm not going to ravish you until we get home or at least to the car.' He drew in a breath that wasn't as steady as he'd like. 'You're going to show that witch and her ilk you don't give a damn for her empty insults because you're far superior to her in every way. Besides, you've got the most powerful, wealthy, scary man in Sydney wrapped around your little finger.'

'Donato?' She blinked and her mouth wobbled. 'Don't be kind to me. You don't need to pretend.'

The look on her face broke something Donato couldn't even name. He found himself hauling her in, kissing her, hard and thoroughly, on that ripe mouth till he felt her turn pliant. Then he made himself pull back, telling himself restraint was good for the soul.

'Our situation isn't simple, Ella.' Not for the first time he wished they'd met under different circumstances. 'But *this* is real. You're the woman I want.' He dragged in another breath and straightened his jacket, pretending the stark truth of those words didn't make his heart drum faster. 'Now come in before I change my mind and take you to the nearest bed.'

For a moment she said nothing, just stared, her head tilted to one side as the half-time bells fell silent.

Finally she slipped her arm through his. Donato was surprised at the rush of unfamiliar feeling that simple gesture evoked.

'You're wrong, you know,' she murmured as they entered the theatre side by side. 'You might be powerful but you're not really scary. Not when you can be so nice.'

Donato almost stumbled. *Nice!* If only she knew.

'You're sure you're okay, Ella? I know Dad when he wants something. I've never seen him so worked up as that last day I was in Sydney.'

Over the long-distance connection Ella heard the shudder in her sister's voice. Despite Fuzz's privileged position as their father's favourite, she'd suffered too, living with Reg Sanderson. They all had. But it was something the three siblings had learned to keep to themselves. Put on a public face and hide what you feel.

Ella looked across Donato's beautiful garden to the dark waters of the Pacific.

'He's not bothering me now.' Donato had seen to that and, despite her concerns about this sham engagement, it was wonderful not to have to deal with her father.

'You need to be careful. Dad's desperate. He

couldn't be persuaded, and you know I can usually bring him around eventually.'

Ella had always envied Fuzz that ability. Ella had never been able to satisfy or soothe him.

'He was so set on marriage! I couldn't marry some stranger now I have Matthew.'

'You're really in love, then?' Even now, the idea of her sister committed to one man took some getting used to.

Fuzz laughed. Not her usual light laugh. This was husky and somehow more real. 'I am. Matthew's wonderful, so capable and practical. When there's a problem he doesn't shout, he just fixes it. He's kind and tender and…caring. And he thinks I've got *talent*, Ella. Real talent!'

'Of course you have. We all know that. You're a natural with colour and design.'

There was silence on the line. It lasted so long Ella wondered if the connection had dropped out. 'I should have stuck to that design course years ago, shouldn't I? Instead of taking off to the Caribbean for a couple of months.'

Ella shifted the phone, frowning. She'd never heard her sister regretful. She knew Fuzz had changed but hadn't expected this.

'There's nothing stopping you doing one now.'

'Ever the pragmatist, sis. I knew I could rely on you for a sensible response.'

Ella felt a pinprick of hurt. That was her. Always the pragmatic, mundane one who worried about consequences and responsibilities. Not the pretty, appealing one. Except when she was with Donato. He almost convinced her—

'I don't deserve you, sis. You're in this mess because I did a runner rather than face this Salazar guy.' Fuzz sighed. 'I wish I was as strong and sure as you. I always wanted to be…purposeful but I'm as weak as water. Even when we were kids you were the one with integrity and grit.'

'Fuzz?' Was this her nothing-can-faze-me sister?

'Don't sound surprised. You know it's true.'

Ella sank into a poolside chair, her legs unsteady. 'You're confusing mundane with strong. I just never lived up to expectations so I had to find my own way.'

'*Don't!* You've listened to Dad too much. He hated that you stood up to him. Why do you think he always found fault? Because you challenged him. I wish I'd learned to do that sooner. Getting away from him was the best thing I ever did.'

Ella brushed back the hair that had escaped her high ponytail. Typically her attempt at casual chic was a disaster, with strands of hair dangling around her face.

'I'm glad you did, Fuzz. You deserve this chance. Rob too.'

'You think?' Her sister paused. 'I don't deserve to have you fighting my battles. But I won't give up Matthew for some ex-con Dad wants to impress.'

'He's more than an ex-con! Or one of Dad's usual business sharks.'

Silence followed Ella's words and she felt her heart thud against her ribs. Donato stood head and shoulders above her father and his sort. Despite the way he wielded his immense power, despite the threat he still represented to her family, he continually surprised her with his compassion and humour.

Then there was the way he made her feel—attractive, as if he saw something no one else saw. He challenged her and revelled in her response when she stood up to him.

'Are you *sure* you're okay, sis? If you need me, I'll come back. You're brave and beautiful and you always have an answer when things go wrong, but you don't have to do this alone.'

Ella blinked. Fuzz coming to her aid? Calling her beautiful? She swallowed hard. 'There's no need to butter me up. I know I'm not—'

'You *are*! The question is—do you want me there?'

'No. Stay there. Has the money come through? Dad promised he'd repay Rob's money.'

'Some of it. Enough to keep us at the renovations. But there's still a hefty chunk missing. Without that the resort's doomed.'

As Ella had suspected—their father was in no hurry to return all the funds he'd misappropriated. They could call in the police but that wouldn't help if Reg Sanderson was declared bankrupt.

'I'll find a way to make him pay it back.' Until she did she was caught, rejecting an arranged marriage but at the same time unable to walk away completely for fear Rob would never see his money.

And in the meantime she was enjoying the most intense, amazing relationship of her life with the man she refused to marry!

She'd never marry to grease the wheels of her father's schemes. Even if Donato was the only man she'd ever felt this way about. She was on the brink of giving in and moving in with him. Because she wanted him, not because of her father's schemes.

'Can you make Dad pay it back?' Hope and fear warred in her sister's voice.

'Don't worry, Fuzz. I'm his ace in the hole. He

needs me for this deal. I'll sort it so Rob gets his money and you get to stay with Matthew.'

Footsteps sounded on the flagstones. It was Donato, watching her. How much had he heard?

'I have to go.' Ella turned away, lowering her voice. 'Thanks for calling, and for the offer to come back… That means a lot.' Her throat tightened. The Sanderson siblings had each found their own way of coping with their father. Fuzz's approach had been self-absorption.

'Okay. I should get back to this painting. I promised Matthew I'd finish this room today. But remember, if you need me, I can be there in a day.'

Fuzz, painting? When would wonders cease?

Ella pressed her lips together as she ended the call. She felt wobbly. Because of her sister's concern. Because of her offer to come back. Because Ella had felt a bond with Fuzz she hadn't experienced in years. With Rob, yes, but not with her sister. Ella had always lived in the shade cast by Fuzz's bright personality. It had never occurred to her that Fuzz wanted to be like *her*.

CHAPTER TWELVE

'EVERYTHING ALL RIGHT?'

Donato stopped beside her and Ella had a disturbingly appealing view of powerful hands and muscled thighs in faded denim. She stood. Her sister's revelations had thrown her and she needed time to digest them, consider how to get the rest of Rob's money from their father.

But thinking clearly with Donato near was a big ask. Look what had happened at the theatre last night. He'd kissed her and she'd begun to believe…

'Of course. Everything's fine.'

One ebony eyebrow slanted up, reminding her of the superior way he'd regarded her that very first night. Before they'd become lovers.

A weight punched hard and low in her belly. Her conscience. She'd let him distract her from her purpose. She was supposed to be helping her siblings. Yet for weeks she'd been too busy discovering passion and pleasure with Donato. It was time she got back on track—faced down her father.

'Something's weighing on you.'

The gentle probing stiffened Ella's shoulders. She'd grown so close to Donato, her instinct was to share her problems with him.

Yet he was part of the problem!

This farcical situation was doing her head in. Her father insisted he couldn't repay the money till after the wedding. Meanwhile she was sleeping with Donato, not through coercion, but because she wanted him as she'd never wanted any man.

Ella rubbed her forehead. 'I have things to sort out.'

'Family things? To do with your brother?' Donato moved closer, his gaze intent. 'Something to do with money?'

Ella's head reared back. He *had* heard.

Again she felt that impulse to spill her worries. But if she revealed her father had stolen from his own son that would stymie his business deal with Donato, for how could Donato trust such a man? And if the deal didn't proceed, Rob wouldn't get his money.

'That was a private conversation.'

Donato's face changed. From concern his expression hardened, setting in severe lines. The spark vanished from his gaze, replaced by a coolness she felt like a blast of arctic air. She hadn't seen him look like that since the night they met.

'You don't trust me?' The words were silky smooth so she must have imagined the hint of hurt in them. Donato didn't do hurt. He was strong, always in control.

Ella breathed deep, torn between duty and desire.

And guilt. Last night he'd stood up for her and her heart had sung.

But she *couldn't* tell him, not if she was to help her siblings. 'You don't tell me everything about your life. You guard yourself so no one can get really close. But do I get upset when you don't let me in?'

He stepped near, engulfing her with his heat and his sheer presence. The delicious skin scent that was his alone filled her nostrils.

'I don't know? Do you?' The deep cadence of his voice mesmerised her. She wanted—

Sucking in a sharp breath, she moved back.

He moved with her.

'Do you, Ella? Is that what's bothering you? Because I don't share every tiny detail of my life? You want my secrets and my soul as well as my body and my money?'

At the unexpected insult hurt crested. Unbelievably Ella saw her hand rise with it.

Stunned, she felt juddering shock radiate through her as Donato caught her wrist centimetres from his face. She hadn't even registered the intention to strike him.

He held her hand high, drawing her closer, and she planted her other palm on his chest for balance. Beneath her touch his heart tapped an even rhythm, only fractionally quicker than usual. Nothing, it seemed, fazed Donato. Meanwhile her heart slammed hard and fast. Her breath came in uneven gasps.

'I don't want your money,' she whispered through clenched teeth. 'You know that.' How could he *say* that when last night he'd been so understanding, so wonderful? She'd never felt more lost and confused.

'Are you sure?' Eyes like the sea, fathoms deep and merciless, held hers.

Heat scored Ella's cheeks. He was right. She wanted his funds to prop up her father's business so Reg Sanderson could repay the money he'd stolen. She looked away, ashamed to be her father's advocate. It went against the grain not to tell Donato the sort of man he did business with. By keeping quiet surely she was culpable?

'Are you going to tell me, Ella?'

She shut her eyes against the temptation to spill everything, all her worries. But a lifetime's hard-won lessons stiffened her spine. She shook her head.

'You don't trust me.'

Her eyes snapped open. Donato's face had softened. That stark coldness was gone as he lowered their clasped hands. He looked disappointed rather than angry.

'There are some things you can't fix so easily.'

She thought of the donation Donato had made to the community centre her clients used. She'd mentioned its difficulty in getting funds to improve wheelchair access. The following day a donation had arrived, enough to upgrade the facilities and more. She'd traced the payment to Donato.

Then there was Binh, the gardener here. Ella had chatted with him about the beautiful landscaping and the flowers. He'd told her how, when his wife lost her job in a florist shop, Donato had given her an interest-free loan to start her own business when the banks wouldn't take the risk.

Donato quietly set about helping people, solving their problems.

He couldn't fix this.

'I'm sorry.' She swallowed hard. 'I shouldn't have lashed out. I don't know what's got into me.'

'You're upset.'

Ella shook her head. Why should her sister's call upset her? They were closer than they'd been in years. And yet she did feel…off balance. Because they'd dredged the depths of their dysfunctional family, stirring emotions she'd tried to put a lid on for years.

'Come on, Ella. Walk with me.' To her surprise Donato tucked her hand in his arm, drawing her close. She went with him. Her emotions might be a jumbled mess but she was honest enough to know it was what she wanted.

They'd reached the clifftop when he spoke. 'I shouldn't have reacted like that when you refused to tell me your problems. I apologise. That crack about you wanting my money was low.'

Ella's head snapped round. An apology? *She'd* been the one to take a swing at him! 'I shouldn't have lost my cool. I'm sorry. My behaviour was appalling. I just… I hate feeling I'm not in control.'

'That's how you feel?' No anger in his eyes now.

This was the Donato she'd grown close to, so close it was tough remembering all that stood between them.

'I like to understand what's going on and make my own decisions. With you, with *us*, it's like I'm on a runaway train. It's racing ahead but I don't know where or why. All I can do is hold on and hope for the best.' The words spilled out. Ella hadn't meant to reveal so much. Yet increasingly she wanted to smash down all the barriers and…

What? Share everything with him? As if he wasn't just a temporary lover? As if they weren't on opposite sides because of her father's machinations?

As if she and Donato could be…important to each other?

'I understand. I used to hate feeling powerless. I was determined to take control of my life and shape it how I wanted.'

'I can't imagine you powerless.' Donato was purposeful, definite. That had appealed from the first.

His laugh was short and hard. 'You have no idea.'

'No, I don't.'

'But you want to know.' His gaze was needle-sharp.

Ella nodded.

'It's not enough that we share our bodies and all our private time? That you know my politics and my taste in films and sport and anything else you want to talk about?'

Ella turned to brace her hands on the rock wall topping the cliff, searching for the right words. She shared more with Donato than she ever had with any man. Yet still she wanted…needed more.

'You know my father,' she said eventually. 'Where I grew up. Plus I tell you about my work.' Donato's interest had amazed her and his concern for her safety had been genuine. He rang every day after her last appointment to check she was okay. 'All I really know about your past is what I read in the press the night we met and the little you told me about Jack.'

His lips thinned. 'You want the story behind the headlines?' His tone was harsh, almost jeering, like his words just before she'd lashed out at him. What was it about his past that made him protect it so aggressively?

'Is it a crime to want to know you better?'

She looked up into that proud, scarred, implacable face, sensing turmoil. Was it really too much to ask? She couldn't shake the feeling that the real man remained hidden, despite the intimacies they shared.

'Everyone who's wanted to know more has only been after cheap thrills, mixing with the tame ex-con.' The words lashed her.

'I'm not everyone, Donato.'

Meeting his challenging stare, doubt assailed her. Was she wrong? Was she alone in thinking they shared something more than sex? Donato's eyes had that horrible blank look and she knew he deliberately shut her out.

So…he'd confirmed it. She was just a sexual diversion. There was nothing profound about what they shared. She'd been misled by her own silly yearnings.

Her stomach swooped and she turned away.

'Wait.' He threaded his fingers through hers.

Ella stiffened. His power over her was scary. He just had to touch her. And Fuzz called her the practical one! If she had any sense she'd run, not walk away from this man.

'I'm sorry, Ella.' His hand tightened on hers and he laughed, the sound strained rather than amused. 'There, two apologies in five minutes. I hope you realise that's a record.'

Ella turned. Donato's face was taut, his nostrils

pinched and his mouth a harsh line that made something twist high in her chest. The sight of his pain did that to her. Her brain registered surprise that he let her read his feelings, but she was too caught up to think about that now. Impulsively she reached out, her palm cupping his jaw, sliding over his close-shaved chin.

Donato's hand closed on hers, dragging it to his mouth. He kissed her palm and shivery sensations shot through her, making her tremble. The way he looked at her, the intensity of this connection, made her emotions well even higher.

'What am I going to do about you, Ella?' His voice was a low burr that furrowed through her insides.

She shook her head. 'I wonder the same about you, Donato. I knew you were trouble the first time I saw you.'

'That's nothing new.' His voice was harsh. 'I've been trouble all my life.' He smiled. 'You, on the other hand, have always been a good girl.'

Ella's chin jerked up. 'How do you know?'

'It's not an insult, you know.' Donato laughed. This time there was amusement in that dark-chocolate chuckle. 'How do I know? Because you're the Sanderson who works for a living instead of dabbling with other people's money.'

'My brother works.'

Donato shrugged. 'That remains to be seen. He's spent the last couple of years on your father's payroll. Besides, you're the one who's here, holding the fort. You're the one your father turned to. The one who's made a career caring for people.'

'That doesn't make me a saint.'

'Absolutely not. I'm not interested in saints.' Donato trailed a finger from her jaw, down her throat to her breast. Instantly Ella's breath stalled as her body softened, need rising.

It took far too long to break from his sensual spell and step away. Ella drew her hands from him so she could lean back against the clifftop wall.

'You're right. We need to talk.' Yet his eyes held that slumberous blue heat that was like an invitation to sin. An invitation she'd never yet been able to resist.

Finally Donato moved to lean on the wall, his gaze on the horizon. Ella stared at his strong profile, still dazed by the upsurge of hormones jangling in her body.

'You want to know about my past.'

'I'm not after cheap thrills.'

'I know. I shouldn't have said that. I realised from the first you were different from other women.'

Different? How? Immediately part of her brain started cataloguing all the ways she didn't measure up, with her less than svelte figure, her discomfort in society gatherings, her inability to charm—

Then Ella realised what she was doing. Fuzz was right. She'd listened to her father too much.

'I want to know you, Donato, and I believe that means understanding some of your past. But if you don't want to talk about it, I can respect that.' She *was* getting to know Donato in other ways.

'Didn't I say you were different?' But he didn't look at her, just drew a deep breath. 'I was born in inner city Melbourne. Our rooms were cramped and I played indoors or in back alleys. When I was tiny I always saw the sky in little slices between buildings. That's given me a love of wide-open spaces.'

Ella nodded. He'd said as much before.

'I lived with my mother. I never knew my father.'

'That must have been hard.' True, she'd have been happier without her father in her life, but that wasn't the case for everyone.

There was so much tension in the bunched muscles of Donato's shoulder and arm she almost reached out, but something held her back. Then he turned and the look in his eyes fixed her to the spot.

'Harder than you can imagine. My mother was a prostitute. She had no idea who my father was and didn't want to know.'

Ella blinked, shock blasting her.

'Apparently by the time the brothel owners found out she was pregnant it was too late for a safe abortion. She'd hidden it as long as possible because, strange as it seems, she wanted to keep me.' The shadow of a smile crossed his face. 'She believed a baby was a blessing. That's why she named me Donato—a gift. Luckily it turned out some of the punters liked pregnant woman so she got to keep me.'

'Your mother told you that?' Ella couldn't keep the horror from her voice.

Donato shook his head. 'I overheard her talking about it when I was older.'

Ella sagged against the waist-high wall. Was it her imagination or had he implied her mother might have been forced into an abortion otherwise?

'When I was six Jack took us away from the city. He was a client of my mother's and he fell in love with her, even agreed to take me on too. He smuggled us away and we lived with him for years in an old house with a vegetable garden out the back and a climbing tree at the front.'

Ella stared. 'Your mother fell in love with him?'

Donato's expression told her she was impossibly naïve. 'He had a steady job and he was never violent. He cared for her and he was willing to accept me as well.' He paused. 'If you'd known our lives before you'd know how precious that was.'

Silently Ella nodded. As a nurse, she knew how tough life was for many. Yet, despite his time in prison, she'd never expected something like this was hiding in Donato's past.

'Did you like him?'

'He protected my mother. And he gave us something like a normal life for years. I went to school, he worked and my mother cooked and cleaned. She smiled a lot too. Sometimes I even heard her sing.' His expression softened. 'She was beautiful, you know. Really beautiful. But life had worn her down. When we lived with Jack she blossomed.'

'He sounds like a good man.' At least Ella hoped he was.

Donato shrugged. 'He had a short temper and an old-fashioned approach to discipline, but he never laid a hand on her.' Something in his voice told

Ella Donato would have put up with any amount of *discipline* if it meant keeping his mother happy.

'He died when I was twelve and everything changed.'

'What happened?'

'He hadn't left a will and his house went to a sister. My mother and I were out on the street and she took to prostitution again to support us. Social services found out and took me away.' A muscle in his jaw spasmed. 'I didn't like being in care. I kept running away to find her. I didn't last long in foster care. I got a reputation for being difficult.'

Ella tried to imagine Donato at twelve, parted from his mother for the first time. He was tenacious and strong and he obviously cared greatly for his mother. Of course he'd run away to look for her.

Her hand found his on the stone wall and he looked around, startled.

'It's too late for sympathy, Ella. I was a tough kid and it was a long time ago.' Yet he didn't move his hand.

'Where is she now? In Melbourne?' She'd bet one of the first things Donato had done when he became successful was provide for his mother.

'She's dead.' The bald words stunned her.

'Dead?'

He nodded. 'Battered by a client.' His voice dripped venom. 'She died later of her injuries.'

'Oh, Donato. I'm so sorry.' Ella squeezed his hand. She remembered how lost she'd felt when her mother died. She couldn't imagine the trauma of losing someone as a result of a violent crime. 'How old were you?'

'A teenager.' Beneath her touch his hand tightened. Energy vibrated through him. 'But I tracked him down when the police didn't have enough evidence to convict him. I made him pay.'

'That's why you went to prison? You found the man responsible for your mother's death?'

Donato nodded. 'There was a problem with the scientific evidence and the only witness was another prostitute. The lawyers made mincemeat of her evidence and he walked free.'

Ella struggled to absorb it all. She'd thought Donato might have tried to protect someone in that fight. Now she realised it hadn't been protection but vengeance that motivated him.

Or guilt because he hadn't been able to save his mother?

Ella exhaled. She thought she'd had a tough childhood!

'Heard enough of my disreputable past yet?'

'Did you find him again after you left prison?'

Donato shook his head. 'I learned a lot behind bars. Including that I didn't want to serve a life sentence for murder. Anyway, when I got out I heard he'd died in a car crash.'

Relief made Ella dizzy. 'Prison changed your life.'

'Definitely. I realised education was the key to turning myself around. That plus hard work and a willingness to take risks.'

'It's amazing what you've achieved.' Yet her mind wasn't on his commercial success. It was still boggling at his past.

'I was lucky. I was mentored when I left the justice system, part of a young-offenders programme. One mentor led to another and some opportunities opened up for me. I learned a lot and dedicated myself to taking charge of my life, getting some control.'

He made it sound easy. Ella could only guess at the struggle it must have been with a criminal record. 'You must have dreamed big.'

'Always.' His other hand covered hers. 'Have you heard enough?' Despite his light tone, there was no mistaking the strain on his features.

'Thank you for telling me. I…' Ella shook her

head. She felt overwhelmed, not only by what he'd revealed but by the fact he trusted her with such intimate details. 'I won't tell anyone.'

'You think I'm worried about that?' He looked big and bold and forbidding, as if the world could spit in his eye and he'd take it in his stride. Now she understood a little of what made him that way. 'Besides—' his voice lowered to something like a caress '—I know you, Ella. You've got too much integrity to gossip about my private life.'

Integrity?

Ella looked into those serious eyes and wondered. Was it integrity to keep her father's true character from Donato? Shouldn't she at least warn him that Reg Sanderson was as slimy as any sewer rat, and totally untrustworthy?

CHAPTER THIRTEEN

ELLA'S DELIGHTED CHUCKLE took Donato by surprise.

'What are you laughing at?' Women didn't find him amusing in bed. Yet his mouth curved at the sound. Her delight was infectious.

An hour ago, telling Ella about his mother's death, he hadn't imagined laughing again so soon.

He'd laughed more these last two months than he had in years.

She traced her index finger over his chest, trawling down to circle his nipple. He sucked in his breath as desire shafted through him, tightening his groin and his muscles as he leaned over her.

'The fact we actually made it to your bed and we're naked. Usually we don't get this far the first time. Or if we do, we're still half dressed.' Ella's silver-blue eyes danced and Donato was as intrigued as ever by their beauty.

There wasn't one thing about Ella he didn't find intriguing. From her lush mouth to her delicious body and her tendency to cover it rather than flaunt it in revealing clothes. Then there were her smart tongue, her quick wit and her love of her career. The more he heard about her work, the more he realised it was part of her, caring for others. She took pride in what she did, yet was curiously defensive about it.

'I thought you'd appreciate the comfort of a mattress.' His smile widened as he lifted his hand to her breast, mirroring her movement against his body, watching her expression as he tweaked her nipple.

He loved the way she responded so honestly, giving freely even as she demanded everything from him.

Donato pushed her thighs further apart and sank between them.

'Don't get too used to the bed, *cariño.* I intend to take you in every room of this house, and there are parts of the garden we haven't explored.'

He took her nipple in his mouth and she arched high, gasping. She tasted of apricots, warm from the summer sun, and her skin's light floral scent was a heady draught for his senses.

Beneath him Ella shifted needily. 'I like the fact you're so…thorough.'

'Always, *cariño.*'

Except he'd never needed a woman as much and as often as he did Ella. He'd never known such unflagging desire.

He'd always been a discriminating lover—not surprising, given his mother's experiences. But this felt different to any previous sexual relationship. Nothing matched the pleasure he found with Ella. Whenever she gave herself to him it was so good.

Better than good.

The best he'd ever known.

That must explain why he took such inordinate care and time now. Why he concentrated as much energy and focus on pleasuring her as he did on finalising any of his multi-million-dollar deals. He wanted to fill Ella's senses till there was only him. He wanted her screaming his name as she flew apart beneath him, around him. He wanted her abandoned and sated.

Restless fingers burrowed through his hair. 'Kiss me, Donato. Please.'

He relinquished her breast with one final lingering lick and was rewarded with a sigh of delight. He lifted himself higher, looked down into her flushed face and stalled, his heart thumping.

Her eyes had lost that glimmer of humour. Even

the desire he was accustomed to seeing had been eclipsed. Instead that diamond-bright glitter looked awash, glazed with tears, and her expression…he couldn't name it. It was more than arousal. More than sexual excitement. It was tender and sad and hopeful and a million things he couldn't name.

Because he'd never seen them in any woman's eyes before.

Except there was something there that reminded him of his mother when he'd been tiny and she'd cradled his skinny frame close, telling him everything would be all right, despite her bruises and his empty belly.

Emotion scoured him. His chest heaved and tightened.

How had sex morphed into *this*? Donato reared back, bracing himself on his arms above Ella.

She grabbed his shoulders, her legs lifting to wrap around his waist, stopping him when he would have moved further away.

He could have broken her hold, except, he realised, part of him wanted to stay. The part that was mesmerised by the tenderness in her expression.

Donato told himself it was the unfamiliarity of it. The novelty.

'Kiss me, Donato.'

'You're feeling *sorry* for me.' He couldn't believe it. Every instinct had warned against revealing so much of his past. But he hadn't expected *this*.

Everything rebelled at her pity. He'd looked after himself, and his mother, since he was a kid. He'd almost killed a man with his bare hands, before he learned to curb the anger inside. He'd survived prison, not unscathed, but stronger and in some ways more dangerous than before. He had the life he wanted, the power he desired. He bought and sold enterprises with ease. He was about to enjoy the biggest, most satisfying coup of his life.

'I don't want your sympathy.' The words emerged through gritted teeth. 'I refuse to accept it.'

Ella shook her head and shut her eyes. When she opened them again her expression was guarded and there was a wry twist to her lips.

'I'm sorry for the little boy you once were.' She lifted one hand to his face, her palm warm against his locked jaw. 'Sorry too for the lost teenager, trying to get back to his mother.'

'I was never lost. I knew exactly where I was.' Though, he admitted silently, he'd lost his way when grief and anger had erupted. When the keening sense of loss had been too much to bear.

Ella's hand shifted to stroke his scar. It wasn't the first time she'd touched it. But this time she did it with such deliberation his breath sucked in.

'Don't worry, Donato. I know you don't need my sympathy now. You're big and bold and formidable. You're dangerous in ways most men wouldn't dare to be, and most women dream of.' Her lips tilted in a tiny secret smile that made something flip and twist in his belly.

Her hand dropped and Donato swallowed hard rather than ask her to touch him again. The sensation of her light caress on his cheek lingered, as if she'd marked him.

'Good.' He nodded briskly. 'Just so you understand, I don't need pity. My needs are far simpler.' He lifted his hand to her breast again, his touch demanding, almost rough.

Inevitably, satisfyingly, Ella arched into his touch, her eyes alive with the same blaze of hunger consuming him.

Donato plundered her lips, taking her mouth in a kiss that held nothing tentative or gentle. It was a marauder's kiss. The kiss of a man taking what he wanted. A kiss that was hungry and not at all tender. A kiss to banish pity.

Yet, if he'd meant to frighten her into drawing

away, he couldn't have been more mistaken. Ella matched him all the way, nipping at his bottom lip, grabbing at his hair, clinging with hands and hips and her lovely long legs wrapped tight around him.

His heart thundered as with one single thrust he entered her, anchoring her to the bed so she couldn't move unless he permitted it.

Triumph rose. He had her on his terms and it felt like heaven.

Except something had changed. Something about the way she accepted his weight, his hunger, his avoidance of anything like tenderness.

Or was it something in him that had changed?

Donato didn't know. But suddenly he was tearing his mouth away, lifting his head to stare down at her. He catalogued her swollen lips and the reddened marks where his unshaven chin had scraped her soft flesh. Shame hit. He'd been too rough.

Her chin lifted, daring him to read any sentiment in her expression. In that moment Donato understood that, despite what he'd implied, it wasn't just sex he wanted from Ella.

'Is there a problem?' Her eyebrows arched as if she were challenging him as she had that first night, instead of lying beneath him, her velvety warmth making it almost impossible to think.

'No problem at all, *mi preciosa niña*.'

He'd work out exactly what it was he wanted from Ella, given time. He'd find a way to deal with this sense of needing yet more. Didn't he conquer every challenge?

If he'd been thinking straight he'd have realised weeks ago that with Ella he wanted more than simple carnal satisfaction. He wanted her company, her mind, her humour and her infuriatingly independent attitude. And yes, even her tenderness.

'Donato?' She frowned and concern flickered across her face. She sank her teeth into her bottom lip as if to stop herself asking more.

Guilt smote. Was he really so insecure he couldn't cope with a little sympathy from a beautiful woman? From his lover? He'd behaved like a vulnerable kid, not the self-assured man he was.

'Tell me what you want, *cariño*.' He palmed her cheek, dragging his thumb over her reddened lips and planting a tiny kiss there. Instantly she kissed him back, the sweet caress of her mouth on his filling him with relief.

Had he really worried she wouldn't respond after his rough treatment?

No, he realised in a moment of blinding clarity, *he'd feared she'd stop caring.*

Donato's heart crashed against his ribs but he held himself still, forcing air through cramped lungs.

'You, Donato. That's what I want.' Ella kissed him again, then lay back waiting.

'That I can provide.' His voice was a rumble, gruff like distant thunder as he moved within her. Using iron willpower he kept his movements measured. He watched her face flush and her eyes shine as she moved with him, sinuous, sleek and mind-blowingly sexy.

Her sweet-nectar scent was rich in his nostrils. Her ripe body was everything he could desire. But even better was the expression in her eyes. Though she veiled it with a half-lidded look, he read tenderness there. Caring. And his heart swelled.

He cradled her face as he quickened his movements, feeling her ripple of arousal encompass him. She clasped her hands behind his neck, anchoring him. Her breath came in little quivering sighs, shorter and deeper the faster he moved.

'Like that?' He held her gaze, loving the way hers suddenly widened as he found that sweet spot and she convulsed around him, drawing him tight and hard.

As he watched, the blue-grey of her eyes morphed

almost to pure silver, a burst of brightness that stole his breath. His name was a tender groan from those beautiful lips as she bucked high, her hands clutching as if scared he'd let her go.

Heat and light and wonder filled him as she drew him to the brink of ecstasy. He wanted her as he'd wanted no other woman. And he revelled in being wanted by her.

Then thought spiralled away, a fraying thread undone by white-hot pleasure as he fell into that silvery starburst and joined her in oblivion.

The sky had grown dark, the air sultry in anticipation of an evening thunderstorm, when they finally stirred. Ella was sprawled over him, her lips at his throat, her breasts against his chest. He wallowed in the skin to skin contact, the warm weight of her.

Desire stirred and with it something new.

He'd been wary of sharing his history because keeping his mouth shut was ingrained. His mother had spoken Spanish to him because it was her native language, but also to keep him apart from the people she mixed with. He hadn't been fluent in English till he went to school. They'd been a team, a pair against the world. Since losing her Donato had devoted his life to improving himself, building success upon success. That took dedication, single-mindedness and the ability not to be distracted by beautiful women.

Ella was the first to hear his story and he'd expected shock and disgust.

Yet she'd dumbfounded him. Instead of outrage he'd found understanding. Instead of disgust there'd been sympathy and support, and tears in her eyes as she'd held him. He'd felt her emotions rise—not excitement but tenderness and concern. Greedily he'd wanted to snatch it all for himself. Not because the past still pained him, but because he felt…different because of Ella's concern.

'We need to talk.' Her husky words surprised him. Usually the last thing Ella wanted in his bed was to talk.

Did she want to rehash his past? Delve into the nitty-gritty detail? Instantly his lassitude disintegrated.

'What do you want to talk about?'

Ella planted her hands on his chest and raised her head, looking down at him. Her hair was a froth of dark honey silk and her lips were the colour of crushed strawberries. She looked like a woman who'd been thoroughly bedded.

Donato's arms tightened as possessiveness side-swiped him. He didn't want any other man seeing her like this. Ever.

She smiled, that teasing tilt of the lips that he felt in the hollow place at the base of his belly.

'No need to be so wary. I wasn't going to pry.'

Was he that obvious? Donato frowned.

'Okay then. What is it?'

The smile slipped off her face and she looked away. 'My father.'

Now this *was* a first. Ella talking about her family, and especially her father, without prompting?

'You want to know how the business plans are proceeding?' That would be another first. As far as he could tell, Ella wasn't interested in her father's business. Originally he'd put that down to a sense of entitlement, thinking she lived off his money but didn't bother about how he got it. Now he knew the pair led separate lives.

'No. I wanted to tell you…' Her brow furrowed.

'Yes? Something about your father?'

She drew in a shuddering breath that rubbed her breasts against his chest. Her face swung back and he saw the unhappy cast of her mouth, the tension in every feature.

'I can't give you any insights into his business. I know nothing about it, and I'm sure your investigators have been thorough tracking down his commercial interests.'

'They have.'

'I know you far outclass him in wealth and, I assume, business capability. But there's one thing you don't know. Something you need to know.'

'What is it, Ella?'

She met his eyes. Her own blazed. 'If there's a loophole he'll take it. If there's a way he can feather his nest at your expense he'll do it. Whatever the deal is on paper, whatever you've agreed, don't trust him.'

Donato stared up into her taut features, the twisting line of her mouth, as if she'd swallowed something foul, and began to understand.

'It's all right, Ella. I take precautions. He won't get the better of me. The contract will see to that.'

'You don't understand. I'm not talking about him jockeying for the best deal on paper.' Her gaze slid away. 'I'm talking about him breaking the rules, even the law. Don't trust him an inch. He uses people to get what he wants.'

Donato read her pain, felt the tension in her and wanted to smash Reg Sanderson's face.

'Ella?' He kept his voice soft as he brushed her shining hair back. 'What's he done to you?'

'This isn't about me. It's about you. You need to be prepared. I don't understand why you want to do business with my dad but you deserve to know he'll cheat and lie and use you any way he can. If I were you…' She looked away. 'If I were you I wouldn't do business with him at all.' The hoarse conviction in her voice told its own story.

'Why are you sharing this?'

She frowned. 'Don't you want to know what you're dealing with?'

What. As if Reg Sanderson were a thing not a person. Donato's pulse quickened. 'Has he hurt you?' He wrapped his arms around her, lashing her naked body to him.

'You think I'm telling you this out of spite?'

'Of course not.' He just wanted to know what else to add to Sanderson's account. He was sure there was something, probably many somethings. His jaw tightened. 'But I'd give a lot to know why you are telling me.'

Her brow wrinkled. 'You're not the man I believed. You're decent and real and… I care for you.'

It felt as if an unseen fist smashed through his ribs to pummel his lungs and heart.

How long since anyone had cared about him?

How long since anyone had looked out for him?

The rarity of it had to explain this overfull sensation.

'Can you give me an example?' He didn't need one but he wanted to know what Sanderson had done to Ella.

Her eyes when they locked with his were the colour of a stormy sky, her features pared back as if her flesh shrank on her bones. 'He stole from my brother. Rob inherited money from our grandfather which Reg invested for him. Now Rob needs his money for a project he's co-financing. But most of the funds have disappeared, stolen by our father. He says he can't pay it back till his deal with you is finalised.'

'Which is why you didn't tell me about this sooner.' Now the pieces fell into place. This explained Ella's willingness to play along with the wedding scheme, albeit under sufferance. 'He was holding it over your head.'

Ella shifted, trying to roll off him, but Donato held her close. Skin to skin, eye to eye, this was his chance to discover all he needed to know.

'At first I thought it didn't matter. I thought you were like him.'

Donato grimaced at the idea and Ella brushed

her fingers across his mouth in a caress that made his heart leap.

'But you're not, are you?'

Before he could think of a response she went on. 'It's been eating at me. I've seen another side to you. The way you are with me, the things you do for other people.'

Donato frowned, wondering what she'd found out. Mostly he kept his charitable activities out of the limelight.

'I felt guilty, not telling you what he's really like. Today, when you told me about your mother…' Her mouth turned down. 'How could I ask you to share that and not warn you?'

'So this is quid pro quo?' His grating tone hid confusion. He'd been unsettled all day. Unsettled by Ella's sympathy and how, despite what he said, it warmed the dark places in his soul.

Ella stiffened, her chin jutting at a familiar angle. 'If you like.'

'I didn't mean it like that.' He ran the backs of his fingers down her peach-soft cheek. 'I appreciate you telling me. But it makes no difference. I knew already.'

He knew more about her father than he suspected Ella did. For the first time it hit him that revealing the enormity of Sanderson's crimes would have repercussions for Ella. How would she react?

'You're still going to do business with him?'

'Oh, yes.' Familiar satisfaction stirred. 'But with one change.' He palmed her hair from her face, feeling an unaccustomed protectiveness at the idea of Ella growing up under Sanderson's roof. He thought of her prickly defensiveness, her difficulty in believing she was attractive and knew he could lay that and more at Sanderson's door.

'What change?' Her eyes were wary, and why not? She'd been an unwilling pawn in his tactics.

Donato rolled over till she was beneath him, all that delicious femininity and warm silky skin.

'I'll make sure your brother gets his money.'

Watching the light in Ella's eyes was like watching dawn break over the ocean, except the warmth he felt was far more than skin-deep. She made him feel like a different man. A man who might believe in things he'd learned never to expect.

He felt her jolt of surprise. 'You will? But it's not your responsibility.' A smile hovered on her mouth but didn't quite settle, as if she feared to believe. It struck him how much stress she'd been under. From her father, and from him.

Something heavy dragged at his gut. Regret? Guilt?

'I'm making it my responsibility.'

Her smile broke wide then and its brilliance set off little tremors inside. Of pleasure, and relief.

See? He could make things okay for her. He could make her happy and still get the revenge he needed from her father.

'I don't know what to say.'

'Don't say anything.'

'Thank you, Donato.' Her hands cupped his jaw, her gaze met his. 'That means so much.'

'Good. Perhaps you can show me how much.' He basked in her approval, thrusting aside the knowledge he'd used Ella for his own ends. That she deserved to know the whole truth. He'd make it up to her. As for the truth, that would come soon enough. Probably too soon for Ella and her siblings.

He swept his hand down the sleek curve of her spine, desperation rising as he deliberately pushed aside the hovering shadow cast by his conscience.

It was far easier to lose himself in passion than to analyse these new troubling feelings.

CHAPTER FOURTEEN

ELLA REREAD THE NOTE, not recognising her father's writing. He'd never written her birthday or Christmas cards, yet the slashing scribble could only be his.

Urgent...designer insists you meet for a fitting but has sent this...only agreeing to work because of Salazar's high profile...demand you be there Friday three p.m...everything rides on this...no time for selfish games...

The missive turned into a tirade and her empty stomach churned. She screwed up the paper and let it fall. Thanks to Donato's intervention she'd had no contact with her father for weeks and had almost forgotten how he made her feel. Now her flesh crawled as if someone had dropped a bucket of spiders onto her back.

Ella turned to the oversized garment bag the housekeeper had hung in Donato's dressing room.

She didn't want to look. She knew it would be a mistake. There would be no wedding. Yet…how could she resist peeking at the dress created for her by one of the country's top designers?

She pulled off the protective covers and stood back.

This was the dress the renowned Aurelio had designed? He'd conceived *this* based on the clothes she'd left at her father's the night of his party?

Ella cringed when she thought of her uniform trousers and shirt being measured and assessed by someone who worked only with the finest materials, the most glamorous women.

This had to be a joke.

Yet the full-length, full-skirted wedding dress mesmerised her. Strapless, it was ruched to a point at one hip and fitted to reveal an hourglass figure. Feminine contours were accentuated by a dusting of glitter from breast to knee on one side. Despite being fitted, the dress featured a ballooning froth of satin skirt that turned the gown from sultry into sultry fairy tale princess.

Ella's breath sucked in, air lodging like a weight in her lungs.

This dress was *not* her. It was ostentatiously feminine and graceful. Alluring.

True, you'd need height to carry off a dress like this. She definitely had height, but that was all.

She'd never wear such a dress. Even if she were getting married, which she wasn't. Severely she squashed the *what if* in her head, the daydream of her and Donato as a real couple, not just short-term.

Atavistic warning flared as she lifted a hand. Surely it was unlucky to try on a bridal gown for a wedding that wouldn't take place?

Curiosity won out. She'd never again get to try a designer original.

Ten minutes later she stood, her hair pinned up off her shoulders, her arms extended from her body so as not to mar the lustrous satin, soft as butter, that draped her. The fabric was slippery and fine and if she didn't know better she'd think that was a starburst of diamonds, not rhinestones, rippling down from her breast.

The dress was too long when worn barefoot and a little big. She hitched it up to cover her breasts as it sagged, but still… Ella shook her head, disbelieving. She looked—

'You're gorgeous, *cariño.* Stunning.' The low voice wrapped around her, liquefying her knees.

In the mirror her eyes met Donato's and shock

reverberated. The floor moved. Surely there was a seismic shift, not simply the impact of that fathomless indigo gaze.

Ella's pulse became a thud, her breathing shallow as her mouth dried and her mind struggled to believe her eyes.

She didn't want to turn because she knew in reality that look would be surprise and lust. Yet as she watched him in the mirror, her stupid heart imagined more than desire on Donato's face. It imagined tenderness, possessiveness and something yet more profound. Something that made her tremble from her knees to her knocking heart. Something like what *she* felt.

She'd fought it for weeks, the knowledge that she wanted far more than sex and companionship from Donato. That she cared for him more deeply than she should.

That she'd fallen head over heels for him.

Donato advanced slowly, his eyes eating her up. She didn't turn. Here, away from the window's bright light, the fantasy lingered that he felt the same as she did.

'It's just the dress,' she croaked.

She felt more vulnerable in this wedding dress

than she ever had naked. The white satin, the embodiment of all those little-girl dreams she'd never allowed herself to harbour, had undone her. Her emotions were too close to the surface. It grew harder to hide her feelings.

Yet the way he treated her, the tenderness and joy, the way he'd begun to open himself to her… all had made her hope.

Donato stopped behind her. Had he read the yearning in her eyes? Her shiver of excitement?

'It's not the dress. It's you. You're beautiful.'

Finally Ella tore her gaze away. Enough was enough. 'I shouldn't have put it on. I don't want to damage it, but I was curious. I'll send it straight back.'

'No! Leave it.'

Ella's head jerked up, her gaze snagging on his in the mirror. 'Why? I can't keep it.' She brushed her palm down the petal-soft fabric. The dress was ridiculously unsuitable for her, even without the fact she had no occasion to wear it. 'I'll tell my father.'

'Don't.' Donato frowned, his expression so forbidding she swung around to face him, layers of material swishing and swaying around her. The soft, unfamiliar weight of it reminded her she had no business playing pretend.

Face to face she read tension in his features. Far more tension than the sight of her in a wedding gown warranted.

'I have to, Donato. Don't you see? He's still going ahead with these ridiculous wedding plans. Someone has to stop him.' She breathed deep. 'I will if you won't.'

But Donato shook his head. 'The wedding plans go ahead. Nothing is to be cancelled.'

Ella stared. Surely they'd got beyond this. Donato was going to help Rob. There was nothing to fear now. Surely there was no need to pretend any more.

Unless it wasn't pretend.

What if he really wanted marriage?

What if, like her, Donato had fallen in love?

The thought no sooner surfaced than she dashed it, telling herself flights of fancy wouldn't help, no matter how much she wanted them to be true.

Yet, peering up into Donato's shadowed face, Ella couldn't help but wonder.

A knock sounded at the bedroom door. 'Excuse me, sir.' It was Donato's housekeeper. 'There's an urgent call for you.'

'I'll be there in a moment.' Donato's eyes didn't leave Ella's. When the footsteps retreated he spoke again, his eyes pinning her to the spot. 'The marriage goes ahead, Ella. Don't say anything to your father.'

Donato paced the study, the phone to his ear. He should feel triumph at this latest news. Soon Sanderson's business, his finances and his reputation would be non-existent.

'Excellent. You've done well bringing it together.' Yet the words ground hoarsely from Donato's constricted larynx. He felt winded, like that time in prison when he'd been ambushed and only just deflected a lethal punch to the throat.

Gone was his laser-sharp focus on retribution and Sanderson's downfall. Only dimly did he hear the rest of his manager's report. Donato's mind was on Ella.

Beautiful, glowing Ella, breathtaking in that fairy tale dress. Like a princess waiting at the altar for Prince Charming to sweep her away to their happily ever after.

Donato yanked open another button on his shirt, trying to ease the tightness in his throat.

Seeing Ella in her finery, he'd been torn between wanting to claim her and the knowledge he couldn't be the man for her. The chasm between them had never been more obvious.

He'd never contemplated taking a bride. Those everyday dreams most of the population shared—someone to love, to build a life and family with—those had never been his. They had always been the stuff of fiction, far beyond the reach of someone like him. He'd never let himself expect anything so temptingly, wonderfully ordinary.

Oh, he could have taken a wife. But the women he'd known hadn't been the sort to spend a lifetime with.

Not like Ella.

His mind blurred as realisation hit.

With Ella he wanted things he'd never allowed himself to dream of.

He might have wealth and power and a driving purpose that had kept him focused for years. But for the first time, on the brink of achieving the one goal that had kept him alive through prison and through every setback since, he wanted what he could never have.

Ella.

He scrubbed his hand over his face.

He could have her body.

He could have her company and her laughter and her smiles for a short time. But blood would out.

He was a loner, born not even of a dysfunctional relationship but of a commercial transaction. He knew more about the ways people hurt each other than anything else.

And Ella…she wanted him now. Wanted their passion. But eventually she'd also want marriage. The white dress. The family. The settled life. The loving husband.

Love.

All the things that were foreign to him. All the things his birth, breeding and experience cut him off from.

He huffed out a hollow laugh that scraped his ribs. The ex-con as the ideal husband? Hardly.

And when she found out what he was really doing to her father…

She disliked Sanderson but he was still her dad. She'd never forgive the man who took him down. And as for the fact he'd used her to further his revenge scheme…

'Sorry, Donato?' It was his second in charge on the other end of the line. 'I missed that.'

Donato stopped before the glass doors to the terrace, his jaw locked, his eyes on the horizon. Yet it was Ella's face he saw in his mind's eye.

'The plans have changed. We're bringing the date forward. Forget about waiting till the end of the month.' He inhaled slowly. Once he would have savoured the moment. Now he simply needed to get it over. 'I want everything finalised today. Yes, that's right. Today. I'll call later.' He ended the call.

Was this restlessness because triumph was so near? Surely he should feel satisfaction instead of this sense of anticlimax?

As for feeling empty—he could fix that with some new project. He'd driven himself so hard and long over this that it was just the prospect of having no purpose that was foreign.

Donato grimaced. Who was he fooling? The joke was on him. He'd always been the one on the outside, looking in.

He hadn't let it bother him—the raised brows and sudden silence when he walked into a room. The people who were scared by his past. The ones titillated by it.

It hadn't mattered because he'd never wanted to belong.

Until now. When finally, in the worst possible

circumstances, he'd glimpsed the real thing—real passion with a woman who, for the first time in his life, made him feel *whole.*

'Donato!' He swung around to find Ella in the doorway, breathtaking in her finery. The sight of her punched emotion hard and low into his belly.

She was flushed and unhappy. One hand gripped the top of the low-cut dress that threatened to reveal too much pale honey flesh. The other held up the wide skirt as she negotiated her way into the room, past clustering sofas.

With her hair beginning to fall about her shoulders and her diamond eyes glittering, she looked like a bride who'd just been thoroughly, satisfyingly debauched.

Donato's body tightened as he fought the knowledge that he wanted to be the man to claim her. To scandalise the wedding guests by sweeping her away from the ceremony and making her his in the most intimate way he knew. He wanted to keep her with him, not just while he concluded his schemes for her father, but into a future he couldn't even imagine. A future where they were together and he'd never be alone again.

He breathed deep and reminded himself there'd never been a place for fantasy in his world.

'Aren't you going to say anything?'

'Sorry?'

'Sorry?' She stared at him as if he'd sprouted horns. 'Is that all you can say? This is beyond a joke. You calmly announce that the wedding is going ahead and then stalk off to take a call.' She gestured wide with one hand and her dress slipped lower. Donato's gaze followed, the part of him that was primitive, unthinking male delighted. Another inch or two and—

'Are you even listening to me?'

'Of course I am, *cariño.* But don't you think it better we have this conversation when you've changed?'

Her lips pursed. 'That's the problem. I can't get the zip down and I don't want to yank it. Can you?'

On the words she turned, presenting him with her pale slender shoulders. She was so alluring, even more so when she tilted her head forward and lifted her hair. The action revealed the sweet, slender curve of her neck.

Donato exhaled slowly, assuring himself he could unzip her dress and leave it at that. His conscience, or what passed for it, warned that seducing her in her wedding dress would be a mistake. One day she'd wear it, when she found the right man.

The trouble was, thoughts like that awoke the dark violence in him that he'd buried years ago. Donato wanted to throttle that *right man*, whoever he was. He wanted to beat away any man who dared look at her.

He wanted to muss up the pristine perfection of the dress she'd never wear for him. He wanted to wreck any chance she had of finding the groom she deserved because he wanted her for himself.

'Donato? I need help here. What are you doing?'

He stepped forward, sliding one arm around her waist and pulling her near.

With an *oof* of surprise she landed against him.

She felt different. The froth of skirt ballooning around his legs, the cinched-in waist emphasising her delicious shape and the soft pure fabric under his hand reminding him that she wasn't for him. Despite being his lover, Ella was unsullied by his world and that was the way she'd stay. Their time together had been delightful but it was an aberration.

Carefully, so as not to step on her long skirt, he made himself step back. He lifted his hands to the zip.

'Donato? We need to talk.'

'I know.' His voice was grim. This would be the

end. As soon as she knew… 'There. That's it.' The zip slid down. Rather than stopping after an inch, he dragged it further, relishing the way it revealed the curve of her spine.

He bent and pressed his lips to the sliver of bare flesh, inhaling sweet summer flowers.

Ella pulled away in a rustle of offended satin. It took two hands now to keep the dress up and her chin lifted as she spun to watch him through suspicious eyes. 'Don't think you can distract me like that.'

Her breath came in choppy little bursts and Donato knew he'd already succeeded in distracting her. He was tempted to stride across the space separating them and tug the dress away. Give in one last time to temptation, before reality intervened.

'You can't just tell me there's going to be a wedding then waltz off like that. According to my father's note the date's set for a few *weeks* from now! He must have sent out invitations, booked caterers, the whole lot! I have to get him to cancel. This has gone on long enough.'

'You're right. It has.'

CHAPTER FIFTEEN

ELLA LOOKED INTO Donato's stern face and cold shivered down her spine. Cold on the outside, overheated on the inside, she felt a wave of fear.

Donato had retreated behind that old stonewalling expression she hated. She hadn't seen it in ages and it filled her with dread.

'Why don't you want me to tell him there's no wedding? Surely this game of yours is over.' He'd even agreed to ensure Rob got his money back.

Donato stiffened, his jaw hardening. Before her eyes he turned into the man she'd met at her father's party.

No, not him. Then at least, despite his air of superiority, there'd been heat in his gaze and a flash of humour, even if it had been at her expense.

The man she surveyed looked dead on the inside. Ella swallowed and tasted ashes on her tongue.

'Donato, what's going on? You're frightening me.' Once she'd never have admitted it. But that was when he'd been her enemy. Now he was so much more.

'Why don't you get changed? We'll talk then.' He glanced across to the drinks trolley that he so rarely touched and Ella's heart dived. The truth was so bad he needed alcohol to deal with it?

'I prefer to talk now.'

'But your dress.' He gestured and she realised the bodice had sagged to the point of indecency.

Backing to a sofa, Ella subsided with a puff of satin skirts. 'That can wait. I want to know. *Now.*' The need to understand had become urgent. She'd told herself she didn't want to know about his business with her father, so long as her siblings were okay. She'd been a coward, sticking her head in the sand.

'You've been keeping something from me, haven't you?' She'd known it from the first but hadn't pushed. She'd been too caught up in dealing with her own feelings. Too busy enjoying her time with Donato.

Ella drew a fortifying breath and spread her fingers over the plush sofa. 'Come and tell me about it.'

Instantly his head reared back in rejection.

It was an instinctive movement, too quick to be

deliberate, and it cut her to the core, as if he'd taken a blade to her heart.

Ella stiffened. She'd known this dress would bring bad luck. Oh, who was she fooling? This had nothing to do with the dress. Hadn't she known their relationship was on borrowed time? The mighty Donato Salazar with ordinary old Ella Sanderson!

'Just tell me, Donato! I can't stand the suspense.'

His gaze slewed to the drinks trolley then away. He ripped open a button on his shirt, shoving his palm under the collar and around the back of his neck. It was a sign of stress she'd never witnessed in him. Donato Salazar ruled his world, doing what he pleased. The idea of him stressed dried Ella's mouth.

'If you insist.' His tone was gravel. 'It's almost done anyway.'

'What's almost done?' Foreboding snaked through her.

'Your father's destruction.' Donato's gaze met hers. Those deep-set eyes looked more black than indigo. And cold. So cold Ella huddled against the cushions.

'Destruction?' The word wobbled on her tongue as her brain seized. 'No! You can't mean…' She didn't believe it. Donato wasn't a violent man. Not any more. Passionate, yes. Strong-willed. But not violent. He'd learned from his past.

She snatched a quick breath, trying to slow her racing pulse.

'What have you done to him?' She met Donato's terrible blank look.

'I've arranged his just deserts.'

'Go on.'

'I've ruined him.'

Ella slumped back, one palm to her thudding heart. She'd known Donato wouldn't have harmed her father physically, yet relief pounded. Relief, she realised, as much for Donato as for her father.

The consequences for Donato if he'd… It didn't bear thinking about.

'Nothing to say, Ella?' He looked fierce, almost predatory with that harsh expression and his scar drawn tight down one clenched cheek. Yet there was something more too. Something that made her still.

'I'm waiting for you to explain.'

There it was again. A flicker of doubt. No, not doubt. Regret.

Ella's stomach bottomed. This was going to get worse.

'By the end of the day Reg Sanderson will have

nothing. The project we were negotiating will go ahead without him.' Donato lifted his chin, daring her to protest. 'I've also acquired a number of other holdings where your father had interests or, more specifically, debts.'

'Let me guess. The debts have been called in?'

Donato nodded. 'He'll be declared bankrupt. His creditors and so-called friends won't forgive him that. He'll lose everything, including the house, the luxury cars and the cruiser.'

Strangely, Ella didn't feel as shocked as she might have done. Her father had always lived on the edge, investing in schemes other businessmen avoided. His recent desperation told its own story.

'You came to Sydney to destroy him.' It wasn't a question. It had been there for her to see from the first, if only she'd taken time to look. Donato's thinly veiled impatience with her father had obviously been more than a sense of smug superiority.

'I did.'

Ella swallowed, shifting in her seat, wondering what else she hadn't bothered to notice. 'And my brother… Rob's money? Were you genuine about getting that to him or is it gone for ever?'

Donato's eyebrows angled sharply down. 'I said I would. The money is already in his account.'

'I'm sorry.' Relief was a wave of lightness easing her tense frame. 'But I had to know.'

He lifted those impressive shoulders but there was nothing casual about his shrug. It spoke of leashed energies and raw tension. 'I understand. You grew up with a man who couldn't be relied on to keep his word.'

Ella stared, taking in the full measure of Donato's disapproval. He really…*hated* her father.

'What was I in all this?' She waved a hand at the magnificently over-the-top wedding gown spreading like a romantic dream around her. Her nipples scraped satin where she clutched the bodice tight. 'What was the wedding all about?'

For too long Donato held her gaze. Long enough for that little bubble of hope to surface again. The hope that what had obviously begun as a bad joke or part of a scheme had become something more. That Donato had come to care for her. That maybe he even wanted—

'Partly it was a diversion. It kept your father so distracted he wouldn't notice anything else.'

'And the other part?' Ella's flesh tightened across her nape. This was about *her*, not some financial scheme.

'It was the final touch that would seal his downfall.' Yet there was no satisfaction in Donato's eyes. 'I encouraged his schemes for the most grandiose society wedding. Any last cash or credit he might have had has gone on the preparations. His social standing will be destroyed when it's called off.'

'And so will the suppliers who'll be out of pocket!' The scheme was outrageous on so many levels.

Then she read Donato's expression. 'You had a plan for that, didn't you? What were you going to do? Pay them all when he couldn't?'

'Something like that.'

Ella supposed the cost was nothing to a man of his wealth. But this wasn't just about money. Her mind reeled. 'When was it going to be called off, Donato?'

He stared straight back. 'As late as possible.'

Ella nodded. 'For maximum impact.'

Finally she began to see. It wasn't just her father's money Donato wanted to take. It was his reputation, such as it was, his pride. She'd been caught up in a scheme far bigger than herself. She'd been…what was the saying?

Collateral damage.

Hurt scored deep, deeper than she'd imagined possible. Not even because of what he'd done to her father, but selfishly because of what he'd done to *her*.

She'd actually believed Donato wanted her for herself!

It wasn't easy dragging metres of ballooning satin up, especially with one hand clamped to her bodice. Ella managed it as if she'd been wrangling formal gowns all her life. Amazing what adrenalin could do.

'You used me!' She shot the words at him as she stalked forward. 'You made me a laughing stock.' And she'd let him. He'd barely had to make a move—she'd been so busy walking into his trap, falling for a man who saw her as a convenient tool. It wasn't the public humiliation that hurt, but the very private disappointment. She'd hoped—

Ella's stomach cramped and she slammed to a swaying halt as pain unravelled inside. Her eyes blurred as she realised how much she'd trusted him.

'Ella—'

'What was the plan, Donato?' Anger simmered like hot oil under her skin. 'To leave me at the altar? Would that have made you smile?'

'No!' He looked genuinely stunned. 'You weren't

going to marry me. You always insisted you wouldn't.'

Ella drew a shuddery breath. The horror on Donato's face smashed the last of her stupid hopes.

See, that's what he really thinks of us as a couple.

The trouble was she'd begun to believe her own far-fetched dreams. She looked down at the bright glitter on the long gown. Not diamonds, of course, but cheap imitations.

'That doesn't excuse the fact you *used me*, Donato. Just as you planned to use Felicity.' Her voice shook and she snapped her mouth shut while she gathered herself. 'Whatever grudge you have against my father, did we really deserve that?'

She wanted to rage and howl. She wanted to demand he stop this pretence and become again the man she'd fallen in love with. The man who cared for her.

Except that had been a sham. An ache started in her chest, thrumming stronger with each pulse beat.

'I didn't want to hurt you, Ella.' Donato stood stiffly, his hands by his sides, keeping his distance. 'You know that. I was going to find a way to make it up to you.'

'And how, pray tell, were you going to do that?' Ella stood tall, every sinew and muscle taut with distress. 'With cash? Is that why you're paying back Rob's money? For services rendered?' The words stuck in her throat and for a frantic moment she thought they'd choke her.

'Ella.' Finally, finally, Donato moved towards her. But it was too late. She'd come to her senses. She shoved out her hand, stopping him.

'Why do you hate him so much? This isn't business…this is…'

'Retribution.'

'Sorry?'

'Retribution, for what he did to my mother.'

Ella gasped. 'You attacked the man who killed your mother. You're not saying—?'

'That Reg Sanderson had a hand in that?' Donato shook his head, his expression as grim as she'd ever seen it. 'No. Though he might just as well have.'

'I don't understand. Did my father know your mother?' Ella frowned. Was this some misunderstanding? Except Donato didn't make mistakes. Not when it mattered.

'Why don't you sit, Ella?' He moved as if to usher her to a chair.

'Just *tell* me, Donato!'

He sighed, his hand spearing through his hair. He didn't look like a man celebrating the success of his schemes. He looked like a man strung too taut.

'I doubt he ever met her. To him she was just merchandise.'

Something cold and hard slammed through Ella as Donato's words struck home. She had a bad, bad feeling.

'Go on.'

Donato turned towards the window. What did he see? The gorgeous gardens or something else?

'She didn't choose to be a prostitute, you know. She came to Australia thinking she'd be working as a chambermaid in a big hotel. The plan was to send money back to her family.'

Ella frowned. 'Your mother migrated here?' No wonder Salazar spoke Spanish fluently.

He laughed, the sound short and unamused. 'Not legally. She believed an immigration agent had sorted it before she left. She actually *paid* for the privilege. But that turned out to be a lie. She was trafficked into a brothel, brought in as a virtual slave.'

Ella put out a groping hand for support. Finding

nothing she took a stumbling step to an armchair and leaned against it.

'A slave?' She'd read about such things but still it didn't seem real.

Donato's face, as stiff as cast bronze, convinced her. 'They took her passport, said she had to work for them to pay off her debt in coming to Australia.'

'Who were *they*?'

Eyes of polished stone met hers. 'Ah, that's the question. There was the man who ran the brothel, and his enforcers, but there were others behind the scheme. Others who made a fortune, exploiting women like my mother.'

Ella rubbed her hand over her breastbone to ease the painful thud of her heart. 'My father was one of them, is that what you're saying?'

She wanted to shout that it wasn't true. That he wouldn't stoop to that. But she couldn't. Everything she knew of her father pointed to the fact he'd use anyone. He had no conscience when it came to making the money he craved. Her stomach writhed.

Donato nodded. 'I'm sorry.' There was regret in his deep voice, as if he read her horror and shame.

Ella breathed hard, fighting dizziness. She felt light-headed.

'Ella, sit down.'

He moved towards her and she shook her head. 'No. I'm all right. Tell me the rest.' She had to know it all.

'There's not much more to tell.' Yet the starkness imprinted on his features belied that. 'She was kept there for years, like many others, too scared to try going to the authorities, too ashamed to even dream about returning home.' He paused. When he spoke again his voice grated. 'I don't even know where she came from.' His gaze captured hers and the raw anguish in his eyes cut through her. 'Not even what country. She couldn't bring herself to talk of the past because she hated what she'd become. She couldn't face the thought of confronting her family with that.'

'Donato.' Ella reached out to him, but he didn't even notice. Her hand fell to her side.

What could she say? She could barely comprehend what his mother had gone through. Ella shuddered at the thought of being forced like that. No wonder Donato's mother had grabbed the chance for a 'normal' life with a man who had promised to take her away. No wonder the young Donato had been so desperate to do the right thing in their new home so they wouldn't be turned out.

Ella huddled down into the loose gown, seeking warmth yet knowing nothing could counter the chill in her bones.

'I made it my mission to find those responsible for the trafficking ring.' Once more Donato's voice was matter-of-fact, his tone clipped. 'It took years but eventually I narrowed it to two men. One had been under police investigation but died before he could be arrested. The other, your father, covered his tracks better. He was lucky too because several of the people who could testify against him died.'

'You're not saying—?'

'That he killed them? I doubt he gave them a thought. He'd moved on to build his prestigious business empire long ago.' Donato shook his head. 'No, life expectancy in that milieu isn't good. The final witness against him is an ex-prostitute, addicted to heroin. She'd be discredited in minutes in court. I've seen it before.'

Ella remembered that the case against the man who'd killed his mother had collapsed because of an unreliable witness.

'But you're *sure*?' Even as she asked, Ella knew

it was fruitless. Donato wasn't the sort to leave anything to chance.

'I'm sorry, Ella.'

His gaze was steady, hiding nothing. She read sympathy and pain, and wondered if it was for her or himself.

What did it matter? This damaged them both. She wanted to go upstairs and scrub herself clean. Her father's actions tainted her.

'I can show you the evidence, if you like. It's been collected over years.'

'No. Thank you.' Ella didn't want to read the statements. She knew, deep inside, that it was true. She could ask her father, of course. He might not even deny it, might try to brazen it out.

She'd understood for years that Reg Sanderson wasn't a father to be proud of. What she knew of his business dealings didn't impress her, and then there was Rob's sudden decision not to work for him, and his absolute refusal to explain why. Ella knew he'd discovered something in their father's schemes he couldn't countenance.

'Ella, are you okay?'

It hurt to breathe. It hurt to think. It hurt, when she looked at Donato, to see that, despite his concern, he still stood aloof, keeping distance between them.

The truth lay between them. It was dark and abhorrent and it explained everything. Why he'd approached her. A distraction for her father.

An instrument of revenge.

Ella's breath seized as pain pierced her chest.

'Ella!' Donato moved towards her but she put her palm up.

'Don't,' she croaked. 'I'm fine.'

She was anything but. She doubted she'd be okay ever again. But she couldn't bear for him to touch her.

Had Donato seduced her just to turn the screws tighter on her father? To make his revenge sweeter?

Call her a fool, but she couldn't believe it. Donato was relentless and tough, but he wasn't cruel. Their passion had been real. After the way Donato's mother had been used by men, Ella couldn't imagine him using sex as a weapon in his schemes.

But Ella *had* been a convenient pawn in his plot. He'd kept her onside so as not to spoil the charade of a wedding. She looked at the white flounces trembling around her feet.

Whatever they'd shared was over now.

He had no need for her any more.

As for a future for them—her breath snared. How could there be? She was his enemy's daughter. That would always lie between them.

'You look like you need a drink.'

Still Donato kept his distance but Ella read the hollow look in his eyes. That was what finally stiffened her resolve.

'So do you.'

Donato shrugged. Facing Ella with the truth was every bit as bad as he'd feared. He couldn't drag his eyes from her, half-sitting on the wide arm of the chair. Her eyes looked bruised and the bright dress she clamped to her breast only emphasised the pain drawing her features tight.

Yet she kept her chin up, ready to deal with whatever else he might reveal. She really was something. Strong—unbelievably strong and decent and caring. Funny and gentle and passionate.

Her mother must have been an amazing woman to have produced a daughter like her despite Sanderson's influence.

'Can I get you something?'

She nodded. 'Something strong.'

'Whisky? Brandy?'

'Vodka. A double.'

Her chin rode even higher at his questioning look. Who was he to question? Wasn't he craving alcohol to deaden the feeling he'd destroyed something precious with his revelations?

Donato turned away, grateful for something to do. Behind him came the rustle of fabric. She must be getting more comfortable, sitting properly on that chair. Good.

His fingers didn't work properly and it took him a while to fumble the lid off the bottle and pour their drinks.

'I'm sorry to have shocked you.' The words sounded trite but it was true. He regretted causing her pain, even though she deserved to know the truth.

'Here. This should help.' He swung around, two glasses in his hands, then stopped, staring.

On the floor where Ella had been was a mound of white—her discarded dress. She must have stepped out of it and walked, naked from the room. Belatedly Donato registered the sound of movement overhead. She was in his bedroom.

His fingers tightened on the glasses.

He needed to talk with her, find out what, if anything, could be salvaged from the wreck of their relationship.

Except she'd made her feelings clear. She hadn't even wanted to share a drink with him. No doubt she couldn't bear the sight of him. He was the harbinger of doom, the man who'd destroyed her father and shattered any remaining illusions she might have had about Sanderson. He was the man who'd used her to further his schemes. He'd had no compunction about leading her on and making use of her.

No wonder she'd walked out on him.

And the dress on the floor?

He looked at the gleaming pile of pure white with its sprinkle of stardust. He'd seen Ella in it and his heart had shuddered to a stop. Not just because she was beautiful, but because he recognised how much he wanted her.

She was *his*. He felt it in the very marrow of his bones.

Donato lifted one glass and downed the double vodka, grimacing.

It took everything he had not to race up the stairs. She needed time. He owed her that at least.

His eyes turned back to the glimmering white dress on the floor, feeling as if one touch from him would mark its purity.

Ella was a world away from him. What could she possibly want with him now the truth was out?

Donato sank into a chair rather than follow his instinct and confront her. He had to allow her some privacy and dignity while she came to grips with what she'd learned.

He lifted the second glass and drank deeply. The neat alcohol burned his throat but didn't touch the arctic freeze at his heart.

He made himself sit for a long time, listening to the occasional faint sounds as Ella paced above him. Finally, when he could wait no longer, he put down the empty glasses and rose.

The empty bedroom surprised him, as did the leap of emotion in his chest. By the time he'd tried the bathroom and walk-in wardrobe and found them empty of Ella, not even a stray hairclip remaining, a clammy hand had closed around his hammering heart.

Fear. Not fear for his physical safety as he'd felt in prison, but fear like he'd known as a child. Fear that he'd lost the one person in the world who truly mattered.

CHAPTER SIXTEEN

Four months later

THE DELIVERY CAME out of the blue. No note. No return address. The label was typed, impersonal.

But Donato knew.

It was from Ella. He sensed it.

Or was he kidding himself again? He'd put off leaving the Sydney house, even though he didn't have the stomach for a new project here. But he hadn't relocated back to Melbourne. Nor had he discovered anything to capture his interest.

Business didn't satisfy. Nor did any of the outdoor sports he usually revelled in.

His staff thought he was ill. But there was no medicine that could fix what ailed him.

More than once he'd picked up the phone to hire an investigator and locate Ella. It would be simple. He knew what part of Sydney she lived and worked in.

But then he'd remember her disapproval of such

invasive tactics. He'd given his word he wouldn't do that to her. That promise chafed him now, when he needed so desperately to see her.

If she wanted to contact him she'd call. She had his numbers, and his address. After what he'd done it had to be her choice.

Her silence showed what choice she'd made.

Donato wrestled with the protective padding inside the delivery box and swore as he cut himself. He stopped and drew a breath. His hands were shaking. All because he imagined this was from her!

Maldición! What had he come to?

He grimaced and ripped the padding away. He stared. Pain banded his chest as he dragged in oxygen, then held it, shock making him forget to breathe.

Before him stood an ebony and walnut side table, subtly modern in its simplicity. Yet it gleamed with the patina only age and loving care could create.

Donato reached out to stroke the top, then the curve of one leg. The old wood was like satin. He shut his eyes and remembered the lush feel of that white bridal gown beneath his fingers and, even more exquisite, the softness of Ella's bare skin.

Had she worked on this table herself, polishing where he touched? Or had she sent it to a professional to restore? Opening his eyes, he peered at the inlaid top. There was no sign of the damage that had marred the table when Ella found it. He remembered it vividly, the day in the Blue Mountains she'd taken him antiques shopping. She'd been so happy, her eyes dancing with excitement. Her pleasure had been catching.

Donato's hand fell. He wanted that again. Ella happy. Ella with him. He *needed* it.

Revenge on Sanderson had turned to ashes in his mouth when he'd lost her. Sanderson was bankrupt, his reputation in tatters, and the police were investigating him, not for his role in people trafficking, but for fraud. But instead of completing Donato, his quest for justice and retribution made him realise how empty he was without her.

Yet he hesitated.

He didn't know if this gift was a sign she'd forgiven him or a farewell. Maybe she couldn't bear to see it and remember she'd been with him when she found it.

Nerves swarmed in his belly and his shoulders hunched tight.

Eyes on Ella's gift, he reached for the phone.

* * *

'Don't fidget or you'll spoil this make-up.' Fuzz tsked but didn't really sound annoyed. Ella had never seen her so happy.

Even tonight, before the lavish party to celebrate the opening of the tropical resort, Fuzz was relaxed, sure everything would work out. She wore a permanent smile and, for the first time, seemed utterly content. There were lots of reasons for that—having a purpose and an outlet for her creative talent, getting away from their father's influence. But, most of all, Ella put the change down to love.

She swallowed as her throat tightened. She was *not* jealous of her sister's happiness.

'I don't see why I need make-up. Or a new dress.' She fingered the dusky pink chiffon, delicate as fairy wings, fluttering around her legs as her sister fussed over Ella's hair and make-up.

'Because it's time to party.' Fuzz stood back, surveying her handiwork. 'I want you to look gorgeous.'

Ella snorted. 'Fat chance.' The closest she'd come to that had been in the ill-fated wedding dress. Instantly she clamped her mind shut against the memory.

That was over. It was time to move on. She

couldn't hate Donato for bringing down her father. She'd tried for years to love Reg Sanderson but had never been able to. The news of his criminal past had been the final straw and she'd severed all ties. Bankrupt and bereft of friends, he'd slunk away from Sydney, she didn't know or care where.

As for Donato—he'd shattered her silly illusion that he really cared for her. She'd been just a convenient tool. She had no business pining for the man who'd taken advantage of her so ruthlessly. Surely she had more self-respect than that, even if she could understand his determination to ruin her father.

'Stop frowning! You'll scare the guests. There, that's better. No one can hold a candle to you when you smile.'

Ella looked up into the exquisitely delicate features of her sister and shook her head.

'It's true, Ella. You're the only person who doesn't realise it.' Fuzz reached for something. 'Here. One final thing to make the outfit complete. It sits high on your arm, not around your wrist.' She pressed a tissue-wrapped parcel into Ella's hand then swung away. 'Matthew will be wondering where I am. See you soon.'

Ella unwrapped the paper and stared, agog, at

the object in her hand. The light caught its facets, making it shine brilliantly. Ella's breath stopped. It couldn't be.

Of course it couldn't. It had to be a copy. The real piece, made by a world-renowned jeweller almost a century ago, featured platinum set with pink diamonds and onyx, and was forth a fortune. It had featured recently in an international sale catalogue.

Her insides squeezed as she thought of Donato and the fun they'd had poring over such catalogues.

Forcing her mind away from Donato, she pushed the bangle over her wrist and onto her upper arm. It fitted snugly.

Turning, she surveyed herself in the mirror. She looked different. Fuzz had hidden the shadows around her eyes from too many sleepless nights and the flash of the costume jewellery made her eyes sparkle. Her dress was sophisticated but subtle and feminine. She wished Donato could see her like this. Elegant. Happy. Getting on with her life.

For a second her lips threatened to crumple. Then she stiffened her shoulders and turned towards the door. She had a party to attend. Who knew, she might even meet some fascinating people who'd take her mind off what she'd lost.

She was halfway from her cabin to the main resort, following a path curving between lush palms, when a deep voice made her falter.

'Hello, Ella.'

Shock slammed into her. 'Donato?'

He stepped out of the shadows looking darkly charismatic and compelling. Her heart sprinted and she had to drag in a sustaining breath. Donato Salazar in a dinner jacket looked too good to be true.

'What are you doing here?'

'I was invited.'

'Invited? I didn't…' She frowned. No wonder Fuzz had raced off rather than waiting for her. When she got her hands on her sister—

'You look wonderful, *corazón.*'

'Don't.' She put out her hand to ward off his words. She didn't want those lilting Spanish endearments that turned her mind to mush and her knees to water.

Instantly the half smile curving his mouth disappeared. Tension replaced it.

'*Why* are you here?' She crossed her arms over her chest, holding in her galloping heart and the pain that welled there. Her fingers clamped on the new bangle, solid and cool against her overheated flesh.

'To talk. I needed to see you.' His deep voice wrapped around her like an embrace and she found herself leaning forward. With an effort she straightened.

'Why?' It was all she could manage. Excitement vied with nerves.

'Why did you send me the table?' he countered.

That was Donato. Straight to the point.

She swallowed. At the time it had seemed right. Yet now she was too scared to tell the truth. 'I knew you'd like it.' His gaze bored into her as if reading everything she couldn't say. 'And I've got a small flat. There wasn't room for it.'

'It's only a small table.'

She shrugged.

'Or was it because it evoked too many memories?'

'How did you—?' She clamped her lips shut. He didn't need to know she couldn't look at the table without remembering the fun they'd had together, their shared passion, the way he'd gently teased her then pleased her and always made her feel special. Until that last day when he'd shattered her illusions with the truth.

He stepped back, his eyes clouding. 'I see. It reminded you of unhappy things. Of the mistakes I made.'

Mistakes? Since when did Donato admit to mistakes? Everything he did fitted in his grand plan. Even being with her.

'Yet you accepted my gift.' He nodded to the bangle on her upper arm.

Ella started. '*Your* gift?'

'Your sister didn't tell you?'

Ella shook her head, her gaze going to the beautiful jewellery that even in this dim light managed to sparkle.

'I thought it was a copy. I had no idea!' She made to yank the armband off.

'Don't!' he barked. 'Leave it.' He drew himself up to his full height and she felt tension radiate off him, making her skin prickle. 'Think of it as a parting gift. An apology for the way I duped you. It was reprehensible of me.' He turned away, but the sight of him leaving broke her resolve.

'Wait! You can't just go like that.' Her fingers itched to reach for him but she forced her hands to her sides.

'Why not? You don't want me here.' There was something in his voice she couldn't identify. His profile was stony, his jaw tight, yet his words made her wonder.

Was she brave enough to find out?

'Donato.' She stepped closer, her breathing almost non-existent, her stomach churning. 'Tell me the truth. Why did you come?'

He tilted his head back, looking up at the darkening sky as if seeking guidance. When he swung his face towards her he'd lost that masked look. His expression was passionately alive, eyes gleaming and mouth twisted with pain.

Ella stared, shocked.

'To see you.'

'To apologise?' Donato took duty seriously. He'd used her and knew she deserved an apology. Stupidly her heart shrank at the idea of her being no more than a duty to be ticked off his list.

'That too. I should be on my knees grovelling, shouldn't I?'

'That too?' What else could there be? Her eyes grew rounder as he paced close, filling her vision.

'I came because I had to know how you feel about me.' He stopped and cleared his throat. His nostrils dilated as he dragged in a deep breath and it struck her he looked almost nervous. She must be projecting her own feelings.

'Everything is different without you. I can't—' He rubbed has hand across the back of his neck in a gesture of unease she'd seen him use only once before.

The butterflies in her belly became seagulls, whirling and swooping.

'What can't you do, Donato?' She clasped her hands tight together, barely noticing them tremble.

'I can't settle. I can't work.' With one more stride he was before her, taking her hands in his. They felt big and warm and tantalisingly familiar. An ache started up in the back of her throat and Ella told herself not to be foolish, but she couldn't help it. Hope was a tiny flame deep inside.

'I want you back, Ella. I need you.' He planted her palm on his chest, his own hand covering it, pressing it down so she felt the quickened thud of his heart.

'I know you've no reason to want me after I destroyed your father and lied to you. I know you're going to send me away.' He paused and she saw his Adam's apple bob above his suave bow tie. 'But I had to be absolutely certain because I love you. And if there's one thing I know it's that love, true love, is a rare and precious thing. It shouldn't be ignored.'

Dumbfounded, Ella stared up into a face ravaged by emotion. The strong man she knew looked… unravelled.

'You can't love me.' It was a whisper of disbelief and awe.

The laugh that jerked out of him held no humour. 'Of course I can. Though I understand you hating me or believing a man like me can't love.' A frown ploughed his brow.

'A man like you?' She shook her head, still stuck on the word *love*. He loved *her*? Was it possible?

'A criminal. A man whose mother sold herself for money. Who grew up in places that would horrify you. Who—'

Ella's hand on his mouth stopped the dreadful words. His lips felt tantalisingly familiar on her sensitive palm. Slowly she pulled her hand away.

'Don't say such things. That's not who you are.' Her lungs felt too tight, clamped by unseen bands. 'It's not your past that defines you, Donato. You've made yourself the man you are today. You're respected and admired. You're generous and hard-working. And if it wasn't love you felt for your mother, I don't know what love is.'

It still broke her heart, thinking of him as a child, separated from his mother and running away to find her, again and again.

She blinked up into indigo eyes that shone with unabashed emotion. This close to him she felt the tremors running through his tall frame and the racing thud of his heart under her other hand.

'Everything you did, you did because you loved her. She must have been a special woman to inspire such devotion.'

Donato's eyes widened. To her amazement they looked over-bright. Then powerful arms scooped her against him, holding her to his heart. He planted his hand in her hair and Ella's eyes sank shut at the overload of pleasure: his fingers massaging her scalp, his body hard and strong against hers, the warm scent of his skin in her nostrils and the sound of his voice, rich and low, murmuring endearments in Spanish.

Ella couldn't help herself. She leaned into him, revelling in each sensation. In the tenderness of his embrace. In the love she heard in his voice.

Love! For her?

'You're an amazing woman, Ella. No other woman would think that way.'

She'd tried to hate him for the way he'd used her, but through the tearing pain, the anguish of discovering the truth, she'd found she couldn't. Her feelings for him couldn't be squashed, no matter how she tried, especially since she understood the darkness and pain that had driven him. How far would she have gone if she'd been in his shoes?

Now to discover Donato loved her, that he didn't believe himself worthy of her…

'No other woman loves you.' She wrapped her arms around him, hugging tight, trying to burrow as close as possible.

The big hand on her scalp stilled.

'What?' Beneath her cheek his heart hit a new beat.

Ella sucked in air scented with coffee and man and shivered at this intimacy she'd thought she'd never experience again. 'I love you, Donato. I—'

Her words cut off as he stepped back, cupping her cheeks in his hands and leaning down to watch her face.

'Say that again.'

Heat rose in her cheeks. 'I love—'

This time it was his lips that stopped her words. She didn't mind because he gathered her close, exactly where she wanted to be, his mouth working magic.

She strained up into him, pouring out all she felt, hoped and yearned for. And she was rewarded a thousandfold as Donato's kiss spoke of passion and tenderness and wonder. And love—the love she hadn't dared expect.

When they pulled apart enough to breathe Donato swiped the back of his hand across his eyes. 'You unman me, *preciosa*.'

Ella pressed closer against his aroused maleness. 'Of course I don't.'

He laughed and looked down at her with brilliant eyes. 'You make me *feel* things I'm not used to feeling. I haven't cried since I was a kid.'

Ella's heart turned over in her ribcage. Maybe if he'd learned earlier to cope with his emotions he would have found ways to deal with his anger and loss sooner. But he'd got there now.

'I like a man who's in touch with his feelings.' She gazed up at him, still unable to believe he was here and that he loved her. 'But are you sure?'

'About what, *cariño*?'

She closed her eyes as that liquid caress traced warmth across her bare arms and shoulders. She breathed deep then looked into his penetrating gaze.

'About loving me. I'm Reg Sanderson's daughter.'

'No one could blame you for your father's actions. You're as different from him as it's possible to be.' Donato's tender expression was balm to the soul. 'I've been falling for you since that first night. It confused me to want you so much, not just in my bed, but in every way. I've never wanted a woman like I want you, Ella. I want to be with you, grow old with you. Watch our children grow and have children of their own.'

'You do?' She blinked.

'Why do you think I'm here? It almost destroyed me when you walked out but I knew I'd hurt you. I didn't have the right to ask you to give me a second chance.'

'Yet you came.'

He nodded. 'When I got your gift I had to know.' He hefted in a deep breath, frowning. 'I haven't even apologised properly for what I did to you. I was selfish. I should never have—'

Ella stood on tiptoe and planted a kiss full on his mouth. With a groan he sank into her, hauling her close. Every nerve quivered with delight at being kissed by the man she loved. The man who loved her.

'There's time enough for apologies later,' she gasped when they finally broke apart. 'Apologies and explanations are important but right now I'm having trouble believing this is real. I forgive you, Donato, and I love you with all my heart. I just want to bask in happiness.'

Donato's smile transformed his face, banishing lingering shadows. He was the most breathtaking man she'd ever known and he held her heart in his hand.

'Don't worry, Ella. I have plans to make you happy for the rest of your life.' He hesitated. 'If you're sure...'

'I'm absolutely sure.' What she felt for Donato was unique. They were meant to be. 'I intend to work at making you happy too.'

'You already make me the happiest man alive.' His smile was the best thing she'd seen in her life. Yet his eyes were serious. 'You make me want to be a better man, Ella. To be someone you can be proud of.'

'You already are, Donato. I respect you more than any man I know.'

His eyes glowed. 'I've never known a woman of such honesty and integrity, Ella. Or such passion. I never want to let you go.' He gathered her in and she sank against him, her soul soaring.

She sighed as the sound of music reached them. 'The others are expecting us. I promised I'd be there for their special night.'

'*Our* special night too.' Slowly he stepped back, lacing his fingers through hers. 'Come on, let's go and help your family celebrate. I have to thank them for trusting me enough to invite me here.'

'You want to spend the evening at a party?' Ella pouted and instantly Donato swooped down and claimed her lips in a kiss as brief and powerful as lightning. It left her quivering.

'I've booked the honeymoon suite,' he said in that rumbly deep voice that always turned her internal organs to mush. 'I thought we could make an appearance at the party then go back there. I still have those apologies to make. And after that I can begin.'

'Begin?' Ella was having trouble getting her brain to function after that devastating kiss.

'Courting you, Ms Sanderson. I want you to know my intentions are completely honourable.'

'Completely?' Her mouth turned down in mock disappointment, even as her blood fizzed with excitement.

Donato leaned closer. A smile lurked at the corner of his mouth but it was the love in his eyes that stole her breath. 'Almost completely.'

Then he kissed her again and she forgot all about talking.

* * * * *